His face grew dark with anger again and Davinia wondered why she had spoken with such severity. The answer came to her swiftly; she was intent upon hiding her true feelings for him at all times.

"Mayhap you will find this of some consequence." He caught hold of her again before she had a chance to evade him. Pulling her towards him, he held her tight in his arms so that she could not escape. The pungent odor of his eau de cologne made her head swim.

The sensation was so delightful she immediately ceased to struggle, lost only in the pleasure of his embrace. At last, however, she drew away, horrified at the wantonness of her own behavior.

"How dare you?" she gasped, and to her chagrin he laughed. "Have you forgotten your bride-to-be?"

His laughter faded and his eyes seemed to grow very dark. "I have forgotten nothing."

Other Fawcett Books
by Rachelle Edwards:

FORTUNE'S CHILD

THE MARRIAGE BARGAIN

RACHELLE EDWARDS

DANGEROUS DANDY

FAWCETT CREST • NEW YORK

A Fawcett Crest Book
Published by Ballantine Books
Copyright © 1983 by Rachelle Edwards
First Published in Great Britain 1983

ISBN 0-449-20906-7

This edition published by arrangement with Robert Hale Ltd.

Manufactured in the United States of America

First Ballantine Books Edition: March 1986

PART ONE

Prelude

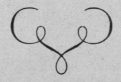

ONE

The walls of the little stone cottage situated on the edge of the village of Hindlesham reverberated with the sound of spinet music. The sitting room of the cottage was furnished simply and rather shabbily, but it was cosy on a freezing cold winter's day.

As the last note died away it was followed by polite applause. Lady Honoria Hindlesham, clad in a warm velvet gown and matching pelisse, put her hands together in the most genteel manner and smiled magnanimously.

"That was most accomplished," she declared.

Her son, Sir George, sitting in an old-fashioned wing-chair agreed. "Excellent, my dear Miss Winterton. I have rarely heard such delicacy of touch."

He was a handsome young man, some six feet tall and broad shouldered. His apparel was of the latest mode and obtained at great expense from Weston of Bond Street, but his dandified appearance was totally at odds with his bluff complexion and he always appeared more a rustic than the Corinthian he would like to be.

The object of their approval, Davinia Winterton, a slightly built young woman of some nineteen years, blushed at their approval. Her rosy cheeks became even more pink and her dark eyes glowed with pleasure. As she moved away from the spinet her chestnut brown curls danced about her cheeks. Her chintz gown was a trifle shabby and several seasons outmoded but that did not cloud Sir George's admiration of her.

"How condescending you are," she murmured demurely as Sir George's eyes followed her every movement.

She glanced towards the only other occupant of the room, an elderly gentleman whose pasty complexion and shrivelled features proclaimed him a chronic invalid. He was reclining on a day bed, a shawl about his thin shoulders and a blanket covering his knees.

"It is so kind of you to call," John Winterton told his visitors in a breathless voice which trailed off into a cough. "We receive so few visitors, especially since . . ."

"Tush!" was Lady Hindlesham's hasty reply. "It is always a pleasure to see you, Mr Winterton, and of course dear Miss Winterton. It is so sad you can no longer visit us at Hindlesham Park. Mayhap when the weather becomes a trifle more clement than of late."

Davinia's eyes caught those of Sir George who was still gazing at her admiringly, something he was wont to do, and she looked away quickly, blushing as she did so.

"I fear that an improvement to the weather will make no odds, my lady. This cursed weakness refuses to abate, but I live in hope."

"Nonsense," Davinia countered in a rallying tone. "You are much improved since Dr Brooke prescribed the new linctus, Papa."

"Ah yes, I own he is a good man," the invalid admitted.

"I do believe," Sir George remarked, sitting forward in his chair, "your health has most certainly improved since we were last here."

"I am so glad you think so," Davinia answered breathlessly. "I am for ever telling Papa so. Did you enjoy your recent sojourn in London, Sir George?" she asked in order to change the subject.

"Yes indeed I did, ma'am," he responded warmly. "I saw a performance of *The Faithless Wife* at Drury Lane and witnessed a balloon ascent in Hyde Park the day afterwards.''

"How delightful that must have been!" Davinia exclaimed, clapping her hands together. "I should have liked to have witnessed it, too.''

"It was a momentous occasion, although I am given to understand they are commonplace and, indeed, only a few score attended.''

"Whatever next I wonder?'' his mother declared laughingly. "As if men can ever fly!''

"It goes against the laws of nature,'' John Winterton agreed, "although I own the spectacle is bound to be worth seeing.''

"Did you enjoy any other diversions, Sir George?'' Davinia asked eagerly.

"Oh yes, indeed. I went to Covent Garden to see the great Grimaldi in a pantomime.''

Davinia gasped. "Sir George, how I envy you!''

Her father was eyeing her rather gravely when suddenly Lady Hindlesham gasped. All eyes were immediately upon her. She was gazing out of the window past which flakes of snow were rapidly falling.

"I feared it would snow before the day was out. Did I not say so only this morning, George?''

"You did indeed, Mama,'' the young man responded.

Lady Hindlesham rose rather majestically to her feet. "George, we had best be on our way back to Hindlesham Park before the storm grows worse, as it is bound to do. Hannah En . . .'' She smiled rather foolishly. "My maid believes everything said by that witch and she informs me Hannah has predicted a terrible storm.''

"It was so kind of you to call,'' Davinia reiterated as she accompanied them towards the door.

"We shall call again, you may be sure,'' Sir George promised.

Davinia averted her eyes shyly. "Papa and I are always pleased to receive you both."

They were in the tiny hall—no more than a passageway—and Davinia would have seen them to their coach only Sir George insisted, "Pray come no further, Miss Winterton. It is exceeding cold outside and you must not risk catching a chill on our account."

Davinia dimpled at his concern and Lady Hindlesham added, casting him a cool look, "It would be wise for us *all* to take precautions against the cold, and do see that Mr Winterton is protected from draughts, my dear."

"Indeed I will, ma'am," Davinia replied, curtseying low, "and thank you again for your concern."

When the door was closed behind them she returned to the sitting room, still glowing with pleasure. In addition to the shawl wrapped around him, there was a comforter at Mr Winterton's feet. A screen had been drawn up to shield him from any draughts which might possibly creep in through the window which now rattled against the wind howling outside.

"It is true; there is to be the most dreadful storm," she murmured.

"I pity any traveller on such a day."

"There will be few enough, Papa. Shall I have Molly make up the fire?" Davinia asked, adjusting his shawl.

John Winterton raised one feeble hand. "I am warm enough, I thank you, my dear."

"Then perhaps you would want me to adjust the screen?"

"No. I am perfectly comfortable."

Thus assured she went to the mullioned window. The snow was falling faster now, each flake dancing in the wind like a demented dervish and the path was being rapidly covered by a white blanket. As he climbed into the carriage, Sir George looked back and raised his hand briefly. Davinia waved, too, and then the carriage set off to be lost in the swirling curtain of snow.

"If this storm continues I fear we shall soon be cut off from the rest of the village."

"It is of no account to me," her father replied. "I can no longer leave the house, but such times must be wearing on you, my dear. Even your sick visiting is of necessity curtailed."

At last Davinia moved away from the window and kissed her father on one shrivelled cheek. "It will not be for very long and, in any event, I am content enough to be with you, Papa."

John Winterton patted her hand which lingered on his shoulder. "You are a sweet child, Davinia, and a good daughter, but what will become of you when I am gone?"

Suddenly Davinia's eyes darkened, her natural vivaciousness dimmed. She withdrew her hand. "You must not speak of it."

"We must. We have contrived handsomely here at Hindlesham, but my salary has enabled me to put little by."

She sat down at his feet by the fire. "Lady Hindlesham will look out for me," she replied, her voice filled with false brightness, "not merely because of obligation, but from a true kindness of heart."

Molly, the parlour-maid, entered the room bearing a taper to light the candles. When it was done and the room was bathed in a soft glow the girl drew the heavy velvet curtains, shutting out their vision of falling snow and much of the sound of the howling wind.

When the maid had gone Mr Winterton went on as though they had not been disturbed. "If Jack had lived it would have been different. You would not have been left alone . . ."

"Papa, you must not concern yourself with my well-being."

"If I do not there is no one who will. The thought of your future has occupied my mind a great deal of late."

"You must think only of getting well again."

"Alas, that will never be, but I *must* think of you, Davinia. You have your entire life ahead of you." After a moment's pause he went on, "You must not on any account place any credence upon Sir George's flummery."

"Papa!" She laughed uncomfortably.

"It is evident he admires you and, indeed, he should; you are an uncommonly fetching chit. But I feel bound to warn you that Lady Hindlesham would not countenance such a match . . ."

"Papa . . . !"

"Let me speak, child. It is a matter of great importance and a warning is necessary; do not harbour hopes in that direction. You have no fortune and Sir George Hindlesham is destined to marry a fair portion."

Feeling somewhat chastened Davinia stared into the flames. "Wealthy men do marry penniless nobodies, Papa."

"Not when they have mamas such as Lady Hindlesham to ensure that they do not."

"She has always been so kind to us."

"I own that she is uncommonly fond of us both, but I am merely the retired tutor of her boys, not a man of social prominence or of wealth. Lady Hindlesham, for all her condescension, is exceeding top-lofty and would not countenance a social nobody as a daughter-in-law, however amiable she may be."

"You are so cruel, Papa, to say so."

" 'Tis no more than the truth, and if I am cruel now it is only to spare you greater heartache at a later time. Are you in love with George Hindlesham?"

"No!"

"If it is the truth you speak I beg of you do not fall in love with him, Davinia. It would grieve me to see you hurt by such foolhardiness."

She turned to cast him a smile and to pat his hand reassuringly. "You need have no fear, Papa. I am not so ambitious or so foolish."

"That admission gives me a great deal of comfort, my dear."

As Davinia turned back to stare into the flames her smile faltered and her expression became troubled. Despite her light-hearted dismissal of her father's warning she felt unaccountably depressed.

"Miss Winterton! Miss Winterton!"

Davinia had been sorting through a pile of linen when Molly came racing down the corridor, holding up her skirts to speed her progress. Her cap was askew and her hair escaping untidily from it.

Davinia frowned at the spectacle. "Molly, stop acting the hoyden and do lower your voice. Mr Winterton is resting and I will not have him disturbed."

The girl immediately looked ashamed. "I beg your pardon, ma'am, but there's been such a to-do," she said in a half-whisper.

"Then I beg of you take a deep breath and tell me all about it in a civilised manner. I trust the cat has not spilled the milk again."

Molly laughed breathlessly. "No, ma'am. 'Tis nothing like that. A gentleman's been found in Clacton's field. Lying in the snow he was, all stained with blood."

Davinia stared at her in disbelief. "Is he dead?"

"No, ma'am, it isn't reckoned so. No one knows for certain how badly he's hurt."

Davinia looked at her with interest. "It is unlike you to indulge in gossip, Molly, at least with me, so why are you in such a pucker to tell me?"

" 'Tisn't gossip, ma'am, 'tis the honest truth and with the snow and all it's too far to take him to the Park."

The thought of Lady Hindlesham being presented with an

injured man almost made Davinia laugh, but she said aghast, "Do not tell me he is being brought *here*."

"Yes, ma'am. They're on their way. Tom Clacton thought it a good idea seeing you have a mind to visit the sick and Beach Tree Cottage is nearest, you see. Young Willie Clacton's run on ahead of his dad to warn us."

"How kind of him. Visiting the sick is one thing, nursing quite another."

The girl's eyes grew wide. "Shall I tell Willie they'll have to go somewhere else?"

Davinia sighed deeply. "No, no, I cannot in all conscience allow that. Give Willie sixpence and tell him to go for Dr Brooke, although how he will be able to get through the snow I cannot conceive. 'Tis amazing the man was found at all."

"Mr Clacton and Jim Haddon went out to tend the sheep. Thought he were a dead 'un at first. Then when they saw what it was they took the gate off the field and put him on that."

"Who is the man? Is he anyone we know from the village or farms?"

"No, ma'am. He's a stranger by all accounts."

"How odd. 'Tis not the season for travelling, and as for being in Clacton's field . . . ah, well, no doubt we shall know in due course." Davinia put one hand to her head. "I must think quickly what to do."

"There's Master Jack's room," the girl suggested, somewhat fearfully.

Davinia sighed yet again. "Yes, indeed there is. When you've given Willie his instructions come back here to me. We shall have to air sheets and put a brick in the bed. There is a great deal to do very quickly."

Molly nodded, her eyes aglow with excitement at the breaking of her dull routine. "Yes, ma'am, and I'll put on a kettle of water. Heaven help us! They'll be here soon."

As the girl ran back down the corridor, oblivious now to

her mistress's recent scolding, Davinia glanced out of the window. The surrounding fields were buried beneath inches of snow. Although the storm had long-since blown itself out and the sun had appeared, it afforded no warmth and the snow showed no sign of melting.

Davinia wondered again how a stranger came to be abroad on such a foul night. His business would have to be important to impel him to be away from shelter in such weather. More worrying, she wondered how she would cope with injuries, which might be mortal, until the doctor could struggle through the snow and attend him.

After a few moments she brushed aside her fears and went into the spare bedroom which immediately brought to mind memories of her dead brother. Tears involuntarily sprung to her eyes at the thought she would never again hear his familiar voice or laughter, but when she heard Molly's tread on the stair she brushed them away impatiently and began to prepare the room for the visitor.

TWO

"Well, ma'am, where d'ya want 'im?"

Davinia stared down in horror at the inert form stretched out on Farmer Clacton's gate. He was a young man, no more than thirty, she thought, and it was evident he was a gentleman. His hair curled damply around his pale face and there was a sticky, bloody patch matting the curls at one side of his head. The blood had stained his neckcloth and part of his riding coat, too. All in all he presented a pitiful sight.

After a moment Davinia roused herself to reply, "Be pleased to put him in the room at the top of the stairs."

The two labourers carefully removed the unconscious man from his improvised stretcher and began to bear him up the stairs. It was not the easiest of tasks, for the staircase was narrow and winding and they were intent upon being as gentle as they could.

"I'd be obliged if you would remove his clothes," she called after them as an afterthought. "There is a nightshirt on the counterpane."

"Yes, ma'am," came the breathless reply.

"Davinia!"

She let out a gasp of exasperation at the sound of her father's voice. When she went into the sitting room, first lighting a candle as dusk was swiftly gathering now, he was just raising his head from the daybed. A several days old edition of *The Morning Post* had slipped to the floor and Davinia retrieved it.

"What is all the commotion, Davinia? I heard the sound of boots on the stairs. Who is here?"

"It is nothing which needs to trouble you, Papa," she answered soothingly. "A man has been found hurt in Clacton's field, and Mr Clacton brought him here."

"Hurt? How is he hurt?"

"No one knows as yet, Papa, but Dr Brooke has been sent for."

"Shall he be able to get through the snow?"

"I pray that he will, for if the wound does not kill him, the cold and damp surely will. Pray excuse me, Papa. I must attend him until Dr Brooke arrives."

"It is totally improper . . ."

Davinia was already by the door. She paused to smile at her father. "Papa, the poor gentleman is insensible and like to be for a good while."

Mr Winterton's head sank back into the cushions. "Indeed, you must give him succour and not consider propriety this once. I suppose you have put him in Jack's room."

"There is no other."

"You are entirely correct to do so, for Jack will not be needing it."

As his voice faded away she said in a gentle tone, "I will return to you as soon as I am able, Papa. In the meantime Molly will attend you if you require anything."

"Have no fear; I will contrive. This stranger is in more need of you. You must remain at his side for as long as necessary."

Grateful for her father's understanding Davinia made her way up the stairs. Molly was waiting wide-eyed outside the room from which noises were issuing.

"Did you ever see anyone so handsome, ma'am?" Molly asked in an excited voice.

"I scarce had any opportunity to judge," Davinia replied truthfully, her mind uneasy.

"With 'is rum riggin', ma'am, 'tis plain he's a real gentry-cove."

"That may well be true, but at the present time we should concern ourselves more with the state of his health than his social position."

"Yes, ma'am," the girl answered, appearing to be chastened although the light of excitement remained in her eyes.

"Any news of Dr Brooke, Molly?"

The maid looked at her mistress. "None, ma'am. It isn't going to be easy for him to ride his trap through the drifts, and if he has to walk I don't think he'll come at all. Lazy as Ludlam, my mam says he is, and far too puffed up with his own importance. Oh, I wonder who the gentleman can be?"

"So do I, but for now we must contain our curiosity and apply ourselves to the more important task to hand."

"Which is, ma'am?"

"Trying to save his life."

The girl gasped. "Do you think 'e's had notice to quit?"

"It is very like. Lying in the snow for heaven knows how long is not conducive to good health, and I scarce know what has caused that wound on his head."

"Oh, Miss Winterton, what if he goes off while he's here?"

Irritated, Davinia retorted, "If you are going to be morbid you had best go downstairs. Do you recall the sheet I put to one side for mending this morning?"

"Yes, ma'am."

"Cut it into strips and bring it to me with a bowl of hot water from the copper."

The girl's jaw gaped, which caused Davinia to gasp with exasperation. "We must cleanse and bandage his wound. Now be quick, but first give me your apron."

Molly was even more surprised but she did as she was told before turning on her heel and running down the stairs. Davinia drew herself up to full height as the two men came out of the bedchamber, bearing the stranger's clothing which was badly soiled as well as being soaking wet.

"I'm afraid we've soiled the bedclothes, ma'am. There's a deal of blood not to mention dirt and wet."

"That is of no account. Is he still *alive*?"

"Barely, ma'am, and that's the truth. Lying in the snow is like to put an end to him quicker than hell can scorch a feather, beggin' your pardon, ma'am," he added quickly, looking shamefaced.

Davinia was, however, not concerned with the blasphemy for the situation was as she feared. "Have you any notion how he came to be hurt?"

"None at all, ma'am. He scarce looks like a poacher but then the gamekeepers won't have been out in this weather."

"Perchance we shall discover the answer in due course from his own lips."

"Wouldn't like to wager on it, ma'am."

She glanced at the soiled and wet clothing held by the younger of the two men. "I'd be obliged if you would take those to the scullery and give them to Molly. She will make you some tea. You have earned it."

They both touched their forelocks. "Thank you, ma'am."

Davinia smiled as they thundered down the stairs. She recognised the younger of the two men as Jim Haddon, someone she had seen on several occasions loitering around the cottage hoping to catch a glimpse of Molly.

Drawing a deep breath then, Davinia went into the bedchamber. Clad in one of her late brother's nightshirts, the man looked even younger than she had at first thought and he was as fair-faced as Molly had described. However, uppermost in Davinia's mind was the worry of having to nurse him. Although her father had been an invalid for some time, she had never actually been called upon to minister to anyone who was desperately ill. What she feared most was for him to die in her care before the physician arrived, which was all too possible.

There were bloodstains all over the once-white pillows and on the sheets. On her second look the wound at the side of his head appeared even more ugly. The door opened and Molly, looking slightly flushed, edged in carrying a tray bearing a bowl of hot water with the shredded sheet and several clean towels over her arm.

"Thought you'd need these, ma'am."

"Yes, indeed," Davinia replied, drawing another deep breath as Molly put down the tray on the dresser. "It was clever of you to think of it."

The girl began to edge towards the door. "Mr Clacton and Jim . . . Mr Haddon, are waiting for their tea, ma'am."

"Then you had better get it for them. When you've finished take Mr Winterton his dinner."

"What about yours, Miss Winterton?"

"I shall be obliged to stay here until Dr Brooke arrives, but I'm not hungry. You may bring me a slice of ham and some bread and butter when you've attended everyone else."

When the maid had gone Davinia felt totally helpless. In the flickering candlelight it seemed that the man grimaced in pain, but she knew that was merely a figment of her imagination. After a few moments she put on Molly's apron and with great care lifted the man's head off the pillow to slide under one of the towels. Gingerly, with trembling fingers, she began to bathe the wound, gaining more confidence when it became apparent he was not sensible of her actions. He seemed so helpless and pitiable her heart ached for him. Seeing him in this room brought back memories again of her brother, Jack, who never had a chance of recovery, and Davinia resolved then that she would do everything in her power to preserve this man's life and thus save another family the grief and anguish they had suffered.

By the time Molly returned, the wound was thoroughly cleansed, anointed with salve and bandaged. "It's snowing again, ma'am," the maid announced in a half whisper which people tend to use in the presence of those who are very ill. "I don't know when Dr Brooke will arrive now. It's not like he'll be able to get through and there's been no word."

Davinia sighed deeply as she gazed at the patient. "Then we had best pray, Molly. 'Tis all we can do now."

The fair-haired stranger tossed to and fro in the bed, despite all Davinia's attempts to still him. His brow burned and his breath rasped painfully, but despite that he was strong enough to break free of her.

She pushed back a lank lock of hair from her own damp brow and applied a cool, wet cloth to his. It was a struggle for her to fight her own fatigue although she knew it was imperative that she should. She had lost track of time but the light was fading again. Somehow an entire day had passed by unnoticed. Davinia felt guilty at neglecting her father who was in need of her, too, but she knew he would understand. A feeling of helplessness washed over her then. This man was depending upon her for his life and yet she feared she was losing the battle to save it. One of his long, slim fingers bore a heavy gold seal ring. It appeared to be valuable, the stranger a man of means. Again she wondered why he had been abroad on such a foul night.

Once more Davinia dashed a weary hand across her eyes as the door slowly opened and Molly came in bearing a branch of candles which she set down on the dresser. "Miss Winterton, can you not rest for a while?"

"No, I cannot leave him now. Is there still no sign of Dr Brooke? It is more than four and twenty hours since we sent for him; he must surely arrive soon."

"It has stopped snowing, so perchance you are correct.

Let me stay at the bedside in your stead, ma'am, just for a little while.''

Davinia cast her a grateful smile. ''You have enough to occupy you. How is my father?''

''Concerned for you but well enough himself.''

''That at least is a blessing.'' Davinia glanced at her patient in despair. ''Molly, fetch me more water. Bring it direct from the pump so it is as cold as can be.''

While she was gone Davinia wrung out the cloth again and applied it to the brow of the restless man. When Molly returned she had with her a poultice.

''Hannah Endeacott brought a herb poultice, ma'am.''

Davinia looked up sharply. ''What is it for?''

''Don't rightly know, ma'am, but she says it's what he needs.''

The girl was wide-eyed as Davinia asked, ''How does she know what he needs?''

''Hannah Endeacott knows everything, ma'am.''

''Were you obliged to pay her for it?''

''She made no mention of money but I thought you would want me to give her sixpence.''

Davinia sighed. ''The poultice sounds to be less vile than her usual offerings.''

''Indeed. She suggested we rub dog dung into the wound to stop the bleeding.''

Despite her weariness Davinia could not help but laugh. ''It is as well the wound is not troublesome.'' Then she held out her hand. ''We may as well try the poultice, Molly. I fear he will die without a miracle so perchance a witch's help is what we need.''

''Lady Hindlesham thinks a good deal on what Hannah Endeacott says.''

''Hush, Molly. You must not say so for she would not admit to it and would be mortified if anyone else did so.''

As Davinia applied the poultice Molly retorted, ''But everyone knows Lady Hindlesham waits on Hannah's every word yet she would scorn any less elevated creature who did so.''

''Molly! I beg you not to be so disrespectful. Lady Hindlesham is a fine lady and very condescending. I will not have you speak of her in such a manner.''

The maid bit her lip. ''Yes, ma'am. I do beg your pardon.''

Davinia sat back in the chair after pulling the sheet up to the young man's chin. ''Go now, Molly, go about your duties.''

When the girl had gone the room was quiet again save for the painful rasping in the man's chest. Soon the sound of it began to lull her and involuntarily her eyelids drooped. Images of Hannah Endeacott, rumoured to be a witch, flickered through her mind. Hannah Endeacott and her vile nostrums.

The woman had lived in a filthy hovel on the Hindlesham estate for as long as anyone could remember and she did indeed look like a witch, with long, straggly hair, a sharp nose and small eyes which missed nothing. The local children taunted her and yet they were also afraid of her. Davinia had never been afraid of Hannah and often left food for her, but she was a woman of gypsy extraction and she'd always been treated with extreme suspicion by the local people. It was said she had the sight, and those foolhardy enough to cross her palm with silver had their fortunes told for good or ill. No one had ever admitted to the truth of her predictions, but there were many who believed she possessed the power to see the future.

It was often whispered that Hannah Endeacott had once been proud and beautiful with lustrous black hair and dark flashing eyes. There were some who said she had caught the fancy of the late Sir William Hindlesham and had become his mistress until he tired of her. Now Sir William was dead, the victim of a tragic accident, which many said was Hannah's doing. There was little Hannah was not capable of in the eyes of the local people. Only Hannah could testify to the truth of the matter and she rarely spoke at all unless it was to read a fortune or utter a dire warning. Her malevolent stare was usually eloquent enough.

Davinia awoke with a start, immediately feeling guilty at falling asleep at all, but even more so at being foolish enough to use one of Hannah Endeacott's country remedies. The room had grown cool. The fire had died down to embers and the candles were flickering low in their sockets. Light was beginning to creep through the chinks in the curtains and all at once Davinia realised she had slept for a considerable time.

She sat up straight, gripping the arms of the chair, her startled attention drawn immediately to the injured man. Her heart skipped a beat as she stared at him in horror, for he was lying motionless, his cheeks pale.

The chair scraped back as she jumped to her feet in alarm, reaching for the bell which she pulled frantically. Her trembling fingers reached for a looking-glass which was lying on the dresser and held it close to his lips. After a moment a faint breath misted the glass and Davinia stumbled back, clinging to the dresser. Relief flooded through her at the discovery he was not, after all, dead.

The door opened and Molly put her head through the crack, looking a little afraid. "You called, ma'am?"

Davinia swallowed noisily and then cast the girl a reassuring smile. "Good news, Molly. The fever has broken and he will recover."

The maid smiled with relief, too. "I'm so happy, ma'am. I'd have hated him to die, him being so handsome and all."

Her mistress cast her a wry look. "And if he'd been old and ugly, Molly?"

The girl looked suitably abashed, saying, "I'll just mend the fire and then perchance you'll go to your room and rest."

Davinia caught sight of her dishevelled appearance in the

mirror. Curls had come loose from their pins and her face was drawn and pale. She brushed back a stray lock of hair as she replied, ''Yes, I believe I will now, Molly.''

THREE

The day was well-advanced when Davinia rose again. After bathing, changing her clothes and tidying her hair she felt more human than for two days previously. All her actions, however, were hasty ones, for she was anxious to reassure herself that all was still well with the patient before she went downstairs to sit with her father who was avid for news of the stranger.

"I am so relieved, Papa," Davinia confided gleefully. "His fever has entirely gone and I'm persuaded he will now recover. The blow to his head was not such a severe one for all the blood he shed."

"That is a great relief to me, too." A spasm of coughing racked him before he was able to go on. "I was afraid for your sake; you would take no rest."

"I am well-rested now, Papa, so would you have me read to you?"

"That would be most welcome. I have been waiting to hear you read from the book of poetry by Mr Wordsworth. You may recall it arrived recently. You will find it on the drum table, unless Molly has moved it elsewhere."

Davinia had only just opened the book when Molly appeared, flushed and breathless. "You'd better come upstairs, ma'am."

Davinia was immediately on her feet. "He isn't worse, is he?"

"I don't rightly know, ma'am. He seems to be restless again and I think he might be wakin' up."

Excusing herself, Davinia left Molly to tend her father and hurried up the stairs to find that the patient was indeed restless once again. Not knowing what else to do she wrung a cloth out in cold water and placed it on his forehead even though it was already cool. Immediately his eyes opened and they looked directly at her.

Davinia stepped back in alarm at the suddenness of it. "Am I gone to Peg Trantum?" he asked. "Is this heaven?"

For a moment she was speechless as he looked around the small room and then back to her. "Are you an angel?"

At last she managed to answer, "No, sir. This is Beech Tree Cottage near the village of Hindlesham, and I am Davinia Winterton."

"You look like an angel." Her cheeks grew pink and then he groaned, putting one hand to his head. "If I were dead I wouldn't feel this pain."

"Is it very bad?" she asked, concerned for him again.

"I declare I would not feel a twinge if you came closer and held my hand."

Davinia's response was to shrink further away and he chuckled softly before his demeanour became more serious. "How long have I been here?"

"Almost two days."

"Two days!"

"You have been insensible for most of the time. You suffered a severe fever."

"But how did I get here?"

"Farmer Clacton and Jim Haddon brought you."

"Where from?" he asked with a frown which caused him to wince again.

"Clacton's field. That is where they found you, wounded in the head and totally insensible."

He looked momentarily irritated. "*Where* is Clacton's field?"

"Quite close by. This is the nearest dwelling and it was a foul evening."

His hand ventured towards his bandaged head once more. "What is it like underneath the wrapping?"

"A gash, sir, not too deep, I am glad to say."

"What happened to me? Do you know?"

"We were hoping you might tell us."

He frowned again. "I cannot quite recall. Was I alone?"

"As far as I know no one was with you when you were found."

"I believe I lost my way in the storm and my cursed mount threw me." He touched his bandaged head once again. "Must have hit my head on a stone. Yes, that is what happened."

"You must have been lying in the snow an unconscionable time. Was it altogether necessary for you to travel on such a night?"

"Yes, oh yes," he replied in a whisper, and then he looked all at once concerned. "Were you obliged to nurse me?"

"You must not consider it a burden, sir. I have little enough to do here."

He looked curious and then glanced about the room. "I trust I have put no one out by my presence."

"Alas, no, sir. This was my brother's room."

His deep blue eyes narrowed. "Was? Does he no longer reside here?"

"Jack fell at Trafalgar."

His eyes clouded. "I am truly sorry."

She turned away to hide her own distress. "You must contrive to rest, sir."

"My brain is truly addled. Allow me to introduce myself. My name is Rupert Jardine, and I must continue on my way to London."

The springs creaked as he tried to rise from the bed and

Davinia turned again. "Oh, please don't get up, Mr Jardine. You must not. You have been very ill."

He groaned and sank back into the pillows. "Damnation, so I have." Then he looked shamefaced. "I beg your pardon, ma'am."

"You are not nearly strong enough to travel, and besides, Dr Brooke has not seen you yet."

"It seems to me I don't need his services. You are obviously better equipped than any physician to tend the sick. In any event if I have been here for two days he must either have a very fashionable practice, or be as lazy as Ludlam."

"Neither is the case, sir. The roads and paths are still blocked with snow," she told him, unaccountably breathless as she pulled on the bell. "We have been virtually cut off for days."

He looked suddenly cunning. "Does that mean all travel has been curtailed?"

"I believe so," she replied, glancing at him curiously.

He groaned again, closing his eyes and sinking back into the pillows. "Is that a blessing or a curse, I wonder?" he muttered.

"Sir?"

He opened his eyes again. "I wonder when I'll be able to leave."

Davinia stiffened. "When the thaw comes, if you are well-enough recovered."

He was evidently aware of her indignation and said quickly, "Please do not think I am ungrateful, Miss Winterton, but I have important business awaiting me in London."

"I am truly sorry about that, but just now you must concentrate on becoming stronger."

"Has any stranger been enquiring for me?" he asked sharply.

"As I have said, we are all but cut off, sir, but I have heard of no such stranger in the area."

"If you do, I'd be obliged if you would inform me."

"Were you travelling with friends?"

"Er . . . yes . . . initially, but when the blizzard thickened we were separated."

"Then it is entirely possible they, too, suffered hardship."

"I think it is more like they reached shelter and safety. Do not trouble your head on their account, Miss Winterton."

"I shall not, you may be sure," she responded, finding his manner not at all to her liking.

Molly came into the room, her eyes growing wide at the sight of the conscious man. "You rang for me, Miss Winterton?"

"Another angel," he said, causing the maidservant's cheeks to turn bright red.

Casting him a cold look Davinia told her, "Bring a dish of beef tea for Mr Jardine."

Before Molly could leave, the young man complained, "I'd as lief have some pigeon pie or ham."

Molly glanced expectantly at her mistress who reiterated firmly, "Beef tea."

"I cannot believe someone with the looks of an angel can be so bracket-faced."

Davinia was hard-pressed not to laugh at his impudence. "Your tongue is well-hung, sir, but while you are confined to this bed you must obey my instructions. Beef tea is the prescribed fare for an invalid."

Molly was giggling behind her apron as he replied in a deceptively mild tone, "How can I quarrel with your wisdom after all you have done for me?"

"Fetch the beef tea, Molly, and be quick about it."

Davinia was about to follow her out of the room when Rupert Jardine asked in a strangely tense voice, "Who else resides here with you, Miss Winterton?"

Her eyes grew wide, more from his tone than his question. "Only my father, John Winterton, Mrs Kells, our cook and kitchen maid, and Molly, of course."

"And your neighbours? Are they close by?"

"This cottage is a part of the Hindlesham estate. Sir George," her cheeks grew slightly pink at the mention of his name, "and his mother, Lady Hindlesham, are at present living at the Park."

"How far is the village you mentioned earlier?"

"About a mile. 'Tis an easy walk."

He seemed to be more at ease then. "I don't suppose there is any sign of my horse?"

"Not that I have heard, but I shall make enquiries as soon as I am able."

"Pray do not exert yourself any further on my behalf, Miss Winterton. I have troubled you enough. When I am able I shall make my own enquiries, although I fear it will be fruitless."

Davinia opened the door a little wider. "As you wish. Molly will soon bring you your beef tea. I entreat you to drink it all, Mr Jardine."

His eyes twinkled as he sank back into the pillows once again. "Can I not entreat you to feed it to me? I am still devilishly weak."

Her cheeks grew pink again. "I think you are quite able to feed yourself now, sir."

As the door closed behind her she could not repress a smile. Beech Tree Cottage had long since become a place of gloom since Jack's death and her father's illness. Rupert Jardine's presence at the cottage, for all his impudence, was certain to brighten the atmosphere even if it were for only a short while.

"You must tell me *all*," Lady Hindlesham entreated, removing her gloves and looking at Davinia expectantly.

"May I offer you a glass of ratafia, my lady?" Davinia asked as she went to sit near the woman.

Lady Hindlesham put up one hand. "No, I thank you. I am on my way to see Lady Durrant." She smiled rather foolishly then. "Are you acquainted with the Durrants?"

"I don't believe so, my lady."

"They reside at Greystoke—a very fine house you may be sure. Everything is of the finest. George has been seeing rather more of dear Miss Durrant of late and I have expectations."

Davinia was taken aback at the news, knowing nothing of the matter, but then Lady Hindlesham went on, "The weather has been so shocking this is the first time I have been able to venture from the Park, although I have heard of the excitement and longed to call to hear of it first hand."

"The situation between Sir George and Miss Durrant must be intense to bring you out before the snow is entirely gone," Mr Winterton ventured from his chair near the fire. He glanced apologetically at his daughter who quickly looked away.

"I fully believe that it is and I must confess I could not be happier, but enough of that for now. Tell me about the stranger. Needless to say rumours are rife and as usual inaccurate. I have heard say he was all but dead when he was found. Mrs Clacton has explained it all."

"That is not so far from the truth," Mr Winterton replied. "Davinia nursed him devotedly for almost two days without rest."

"You are to be commended, my dear," Lady Hindlesham told her, "but do tell me how it came about for I was never more surprised to learn that they had brought the poor creature here rather than Hindlesham Park."

Davinia quickly told the woman about the events of that night and all the while Lady Hindlesham clucked her tongue. "How dreadful, and what a pity we could not send help to you. You employ so few servants, the imposition must have been quite alarming."

"We did contrive," Davinia pointed out.

"And quite handsomely, I do not doubt. How is the invalid now?"

"Much recovered I am glad to say."

"But what does *Dr Brooke* say? It is his opinion, after all, which carries any weight."

"He arrived only minutes before you, my lady. He is with Mr Jardine now, but I am bound to say we no longer need his services. I am persuaded Hannah Endeacott's herb poultice worked as well as any purging could."

The dowager threw her hands up in the air. "Hannah Endeacott! That witch! If you attach any credence to her remedies 'tis a wonder the patient survived at all. I had not thought you so foolish, Miss Winterton."

"I am persuaded the poultice did work, my lady," Davinia answered meekly, not wishing to offend the lady further.

"I am not so easily convinced," Lady Hindlesham said firmly. "Did you say this fellow is a gentleman?"

"It would appear so, my lady. His manner, his clothing all proclaim it to be so."

Lady Hindlesham appeared thoughtful. "That might well be, but I do not know the name at all."

"I don't believe he is a local man."

"My sphere of acquaintances extends well beyond the perimeter of my son's estates, Miss Winterton," the dowager replied, casting her a deprecating smile.

"Oh, indeed, my lady. I didn't meant to suggest . . ."

"He cannot be a gentleman," the woman then declared and Davinia cast her a startled look, "for George declares no true gentleman would allow himself to be thrown from his horse."

"The weather was atrocious," Davinia reminded her.

"I recall it all too well. What *was* he doing abroad on such a night?"

"I cannot say," Davinia replied demurely, in all truthfulness.

" 'Tis a great mystery, I own," the lady confided, "but no doubt we shall all be enlightened in due course." She rose majestically from her chair. "And now I must take my leave of you both. I shall call again when time permits."

When Davinia returned to the sitting room a few moments later she said with a sigh, "I fear Lady Hindlesham is miffed because she was excluded from the excitement."

"Indeed," her father agreed. "How dare he be injured nearer to Beech Tree Cottage than Hindlesham Park?"

He was exhibiting a little of his once famed wit and Davinia smiled. Then he began to cough and she looked concerned. "I will fetch you linctus, Papa."

"No, no, my dear. Do not trouble, for Molly brought it to me not long ago." After a moment's pause he asked, "Did you know of Sir George's relationship with Miss Durrant?"

Davinia began to plump the cushions. "No, Papa, I did not. I cannot conceive why you thought I might."

"Only because it seemed to me George Hindlesham confided in you."

"I am not privy to Sir George's friendships. Oh, I do believe I hear Dr Brooke on the stairs."

She hurried to the door and sure enough the physician was coming down the stairs. "Miss Winterton," he began in outraged tones the moment she appeared in the hallway, "I feel I must protest. I have made the journey on foot in considerable discomfort because of the vile conditions prevalent at present, but I am bound to report the patient displays total ingratitude for my efforts."

Davinia was astonished. "I don't understand, sir. What has transpired between you?"

"Mr Jardine refuses to be bled or to be purged, and, therefore, I cannot accept responsibility for his condition."

"I do beg your pardon, Dr Brooke . . . I am persuaded when Mr Jardine fully understands . . ."

"I have never been so mortified in my life, Miss Winterton. He told me to go to the Devil. The man's attic's to let if you ask me. You would be well advised to turn him out as soon as possible."

Davinia suddenly found herself wishing she might have witnessed the scene and was trying hard not to smile, but she did manage to affect a concerned expression. "Perchance, the wound . . . ?"

"That is healing in a satisfactory manner, Miss Winterton, but it does not mean to say the blow hasn't unhinged his mind. Such cases are not uncommon and I entreat you to keep a very close watch whilst he remains beneath your roof."

Davinia opened the door, still affecting a concerned expression. "I will heed your warning, Dr Brooke. Do you propose to call again?"

"I can see no advantage in my doing so, Miss Winterton, either for Mr Jardine or myself." He was halfway out of the cottage when he added, "I really should call on Mr Winterton before I go."

"My father is keeping fairly well, Dr Brooke. I am certain he will excuse you on this occasion and understand your haste in leaving. It is possible we might have more snow."

"Then I shall bid you good day, ma'am."

For a few moments Davinia watched him slithering down the drive on the melting snow and then she closed the door, leaning back against it, laughing as she had not laughed for longer than she could remember.

FOUR

"My dear young fellow," John Winterton greeted Rupert Jardine as he entered the sitting room rather hesitantly, "I have been in a fidge to meet you since your arrival. Pray sit down and if you are in a mind to do so, converse with me a while."

Rupert Jardine, clad in an elegant brocade dressing gown once the property of the late Jack Winterton, sat down in a wing chair by the fire to face his host. The bandage was still wrapped around his head but other than that he appeared remarkably fit. His cheeks had a healthy glow and his eyes contained a sparkle which appeared permanent.

"And I you, sir," the young man replied. "I am obliged to you and your daughter for your hospitality."

"You must not mention it. We so rarely have visitors that even one in such unfortunate circumstances is welcome."

Rupert Jardine laughed and it was then that Davinia came into the room, gasping with alarm as she did so. "Mr Jardine, you really should not be out of your bed. Dr Brooke . . ."

His eyes sparkled with mischief. "That mountebank ordered me abed for at least a sen'night, so I deemed it prudent to get up as soon as I could."

Davinia cast him a look of exasperation. "You are past praying for, sir."

"So I am often told. I trust you will not act the martinet and order me back upstairs."

32

She stiffened at what was obviously teasing. "You are a grown man, sir, and I cannot tie you down, I fear."

His eyes lingered on her momentarily. "No female has as yet succeeded in doing so."

Her heart fluttered as her father said, "You are quite evidently a townsman, Mr Jardine."

"Mr Jardine lives in London, Papa," Davinia informed him.

"The cradle of the Devil," her father pronounced, much to his visitor's amusement.

"I trust you will not consider me one of his disciples, sir."

John Winterton gazed at him steadily. "I trust you are not."

The young man continued to look amused. "You may rely upon that, sir. I am merely a humble man-about-town, seeking his pleasures where he may."

Davinia sat down and picked up her sewing as her father asked, "What brought you to Hindlesham, Mr Jardine?"

It seemed that the young man hesitated before answering. "Pure chance. I became lost, taking what I believed to be a short route. I had been visiting friends in Dorset and decided to return home before the snow trapped me, a fruitless effort as it now appears."

"You cannot have chosen a worst time to travel. Your need to be in London must have been dire."

Rupert Jardine grinned. "Dire is mayhap not the correct word, sir, but the lady certainly is a most charming creature and I was anxious to be with her."

Davinia paused in her sewing to cast him a glance. It seemed odd that he should volunteer such information.

However, John Winterton laughed. "Young men are ever in pursuit of the same pleasures. That is something which never changes."

"I am of the opinion, Mr Winterton, that such matters will always remain of interest to gentlemen. I often wish I might have been blessed with a more serious turn of mind, but no amount of longing can make it so."

"I must disagree. It is merely an attitude of mind and you can pursue more serious matters if you so wish."

Rupert Jardine looked sheepish. "Mayhap I don't desire to do so badly enough."

"Ah, yes, that is evident, but why is it so, Mr Jardine?"

Davinia looked up to note that her father's face was more animated than for a long time past and it was evident he was enjoying the visitor's company. For a long while a lively argument ensued on the subject of virtue versus immorality which she was content to listen to in silence. It was enough that their normally dull existence had been enlivened by this young man's bright presence.

On several occasions remarks made by their guest resulted in Mr Winterton laughing heartily until a spasm of coughing brought their lively conversation to a premature end. Davinia jumped quickly to her feet and rang for Molly who immediately hurried away for the linctus and spoon.

"Miss Winterton, can I not be of help?" Rupert Jardine begged as Davinia tended her father.

"I'm afraid we must wait until the spasm abates," she replied. "There is little anyone can do."

"In that event I had best retire to my room."

She looked up quickly. "I beg of you do not, Mr Jardine, unless you are feeling ill yourself. Papa has so enjoyed your company and is like to do so again."

Mr Winterton slumped back into the cushions and said in a breathless voice, "Davinia is correct, sir. I beg of you remain if you will. I shall soon be recovered and mayhap later you will play backgammon with me."

The young man sank back into the chair. "It will be a pleasure, Mr Winterton. In the meantime, whilst you rest, would you like me to read to you?"

"Indeed, that would be most pleasant. Fielding?"

"Whatever you wish."

Davinia cast him a grateful smile and went to fetch a book from the cabinet. When she handed it to their guest he took it with a smile. His hand touched hers but briefly and Davinia withdrew hers quickly. As Rupert Jardine began to read, his voice deep and melodic, she returned to her chair, surprised at the amount of feeling he was able to express in his reading. At a glance it was evident her father was also enjoying listening to the reading and Davinia knew the visitor's presence was causing her as much pleasure, too.

Davinia walked disconsolately through the garden watching for the snowdrops which were pushing their way through the sodden ground. The sound of hoofbeats caused her to hurry to where she could see Sir George riding up the drive. As always the sight of him made her smile and she hurried to meet him.

"Sir George! How pleasant it is to see you."

He dismounted and, holding the reins, advanced towards her, saying heartily as he removed his high-crowned beaver, "And I you, Miss Winterton, but have you no thought for your health? You will catch a chill out here. Allow me to escort you inside."

As ever she was warmed by his concern for her. "You are very kind to say so, Sir George, but after being cooped up in the house for so many days I am truly enjoying the air. Do you not feel spring is close at hand?"

"The lambing has begun but that doesn't mean the bad weather is over."

She laughed. " 'Tis not in your nature to be so Friday-faced."

"Nor am I ever likely to be when I am in your company, ma'am." She dimpled with pleasure and he went on in a more serious vein, "How is your guest? Is he improving?"

"All the time. In fact he is displaying impatience now. I believe he is anxious to be gone from here."

The young man looked shocked. "Surely not. Any man

fortunate enough to have the pleasure of your company cannot be so foolish.''

Again she dimpled. ''He has urgent business awaiting him in London.''

''Business of what kind?''

Davinia looked away. ''I have no notion for he has not confided in me. Mayhap you would like to meet him and discuss the matter for yourself. I am persuaded he would welcome a visitor now he is so well recovered.''

''Alas today I cannot, although I confess to be in a fidge to do so. Arrangements have been made and I am due at Greystoke.'' He frowned. ''Have you had the honour of meeting Miss Durrant?''

Davinia felt discomforted. ''I believe I once set eyes upon her at Hindlesham Park although I have not as yet had the honour of making her acquaintance. I am bound to say she appears to be delightful.''

He looked away, staring into the distance. ''Mama is exceeding fond of her.''

''Lady Hindlesham's judgement is always sound.''

He began to move away from her. It seemed to Davinia he was suddenly anxious to be away and that saddened her, for she had always enjoyed a carefree relationship with George Hindlesham, long before he had succeeded to the title.

''Mayhap you will call again before long,'' she ventured hopefully, ''when you have more time at your disposal.''

''You may rely upon it. Naturally, I would like to meet your guest, but I could not delay telling you of my admiration. Mama informed me of your devoted nursing. Mr Jardine is an uncommonly fortunate man.''

''If you truly wish to speak with him do not delay, Sir George, for he is like to be gone before long.''

As the words were spoken her spirits plummeted. Since his arrival Rupert Jardine had raised all their spirits with his quick wit and gentle teasing. Even her father, after conversations with the young man, had seemed more invigorated than Davinia had witnessed in many a month.

She pondered, too, on her conversation with Sir George and his mother; Miss Durrant's name cropped up often these days and Davinia dare not allow herself to think about George Hindlesham marrying, or Rupert Jardine leaving. Both events seemed more than likely to occur before long, and afterwards life would become bleaker than it had ever been before.

George Hindlesham mounted his horse and raised his hand as he turned to ride away. When he had gone she went back into the cottage and found Molly hard at work in the scullery with Sarah, the kitchen maid.

"Have you prepared the basket for Hannah Endeacott?" Davinia enquired, glancing quickly around the scullery which had received so little of her attention lately.

"Yes, ma'am. I'll get it from the pantry," Molly replied. She brought it out and handed it to her mistress. "I've put in a good piece of ham and some fresh bread and cheese, just as you said."

As Davinia peered underneath the cloth which covered the basket, she said, "If Mr Winterton awakes before I am back, pray tell him where I am gone."

Molly looked abashed. "Yes, ma'am, but I don't know how you dare."

"Tush. Hannah Endeacott is quite harmless. I was afraid of her when I was a child, but I am scarce that any longer, and neither are you."

The girl looked a trifle embarrassed before she asked, "While you're gone shall I make certain Mr Jardine is not in need of anything?"

Davinia's lips curved into a smile. "Oh, I am persuaded if Mr Jardine is in need of anything he will make his wishes known."

Molly looked away quickly and, taking the basket over her arm, Davinia walked out of the room. However she had only just stepped out of the cottage when she heard someone calling her name from within. Turning on her heel, she started, as she saw Rupert Jardine coming down the stairs.

"Mr Jardine! You are dressed!"

His lips quirked into a now familiar smile. "I did not wish to outrage your sensibilities by appearing déshabillé."

His gentle mockery caused her considerable embarrassment, but she strove as in days past not to exhibit her discomposure whenever he teased her. It was the very first time she had seen him standing up straight, and she was amazed at how tall he was. His elegant brown riding coat had been cleaned and pressed, although most of the wet had been absorbed by his caped riding coat. Even though the illness resulting from his fall had caused a little loss of weight he still filled out the coat and riding breeches handsomely. Sarah had put a shine on his boots, which would surely satisfy the discerning eye of Beau Brummel himself.

"Oh, Mr Jardine, you look very well," she was bound to say.

"It is all due to your devoted nursing," he replied, coming down the rest of the stairs and bowing low before her. Then as he straightened up he took one of her hands in his. "How may I thank you?"

With some difficulty she extricated her hand from his and averted her face. " 'Tis enough to see you returned to health, sir. I wish such miracles could be performed for my father's sake."

He looked all at once concerned. "How is Mr Winterton today?"

"Not very well, I fear."

"I am truly sorry to hear you say so." He did look regretful. "May I call in to see him?"

"I don't doubt he will welcome you later, but for now he is resting."

"So be it." After a pause he ventured, "Mayhap that awful quack is not the ideal physician to treat his illness."

Davinia stiffened. "Dr Brooke is a splendid physician. Lady Hindlesham's own! There is no higher recommendation."

"I beg your pardon, ma'am. That was presumptuous of me."

Davinia drew herself to full height which was not very considerable. "Indeed it was, sir, and now pray excuse me. I was about to embark upon an errand which I cannot delay any longer."

"I beg your pardon for detaining you. However, will you allow me to accompany you, if that is not also too presumptuous of me?"

Startled anew she suddenly felt alarmed at the thought of his company and retorted, "It is a fair walk and you must still be a trifle weak."

"I do not feel it and indeed I believe I am robust enough to endure it. If the good country air puts such complimentary colour into my cheeks as it has done for yours I shall be well satisfied."

Davinia was determined to remain stoical in the face of such practised charm. "Your coat is in the cupboard under the stairs," she answered stiffly.

When he retrieved it he laughed. "This coat cost me the purse of Fortunatus only a month ago. It is sadly ravaged now."

Sensing his criticism Davinia stiffened. "We have done our best to put it to rights, Mr Jardine, but a soaking such as it received that night is not conducive to the well-being of fine cloth."

He was immediately apologetic. "I did not mean to complain, Miss Winterton, I assure you."

He tossed it across his broad shoulders and followed her out of the cottage. As he did so he inhaled the air appreciatively. "On a day like today it is good to be alive."

She did not answer and as he fell into step at her side he added, "I am indeed a clumsy blabberer, ma'am. Your loss is still very recent and I would not for anything remind you of it.''

"I am reminded of Jack at every turn, and indeed, that is what I would wish.''

"You were very close to him, I feel.''

"Yes, I was, and I miss him very much.''

As they set off across the fields a companionable silence descended upon them until after a while he asked, ''Have any strangers been seen in the neighbourhood of late, Miss Winterton?''

"Not to my knowledge. Are you expecting someone?''

She glanced up at him and away again. The bandage had been removed and a court plaster put in its place, otherwise there was no sign of the desperately ill young man carried into the cottage such a short time before. Hatless, his golden curls blew in the breeze as he stared across the fields into the distance.

"In truth I am not, although it is possible one of my companions might return to make enquiries.'' After a moment's pause he added, ''I did wonder about the man who called at the cottage earlier.''

At this Davinia was forced to laugh. ''A stranger? Oh no, Mr Jardine. That was Sir George Hindlesham!''

He was taken aback. ''From all you have told me I imagined him to be an elderly man.''

"Sir William died two years ago.''

"Sir George seems to hold you in great esteem.''

She hoped he would not be aware of her confusion. ''How did you gain such an impression? You were not present when he was here.''

He smiled foolishly. ''You must forgive my presumption, but when I heard a horseman approach I looked out of the window and saw him arriving. My impression was of a man who had a good deal of regard for you.''

"Sir George and I grew up together,'' Davinia told him with some difficulty. ''Papa was tutor to the Hindlesham boys before they went away to school and then to Cambridge. There are several of them and Papa taught them all.''

"My own *alma mater* is Oxford."

She glanced at him again, all at once anxious not to be drawn into any further conversation about George Hindlesham. "It seems to me, Mr Jardine, you know a good deal about those of us who live in and around Hindlesham and yet we know nothing of you."

He bestowed upon her then a devastating smile. "There is little for an invalid to do save consider his immediate surroundings so I pray forgive my interest. I can assure you, Miss Winterton, there is little about me which would interest you. I am in the ordinary manner of a scapegrace."

She could not help but laugh at his impudence and asked, "Do you always reside in London?"

"No, not always, but it is true to say I live in London for most of the year."

Her eyes glowed at the thought. "That must be most interesting. I have often wondered about London and what it is like to live there."

"Have you never visited?"

"No, but I do long to see the opera, the theatre and mayhap Astley's Amphi-theatre. Sir George and his brothers have often told me about all the assemblies, too. Frederick Hindlesham once caught sight of Beau Brummel in Piccadilly and he visited an emporium lit by gas lamps. Do you believe all buildings will one day be lit in such a way?"

"Undoubtedly, but I also believe we shall be using candles for some time to come." He glanced at her as they walked briskly across the field. "Mayhap you will one day be able to partake of the diversions."

She laughed self-consciously. "I cannot conceive of that, sir. There are few enough occasions when I am able to leave Papa.''

"That is indeed a pity, for I am persuaded you would take the *ton* by storm if you were introduced into that circle."

Her face grew red as he jumped a stile and then took the basket before handing her over it, too. As she took the basket from him she retorted, "It is not my wish to be a part of Society, nor is there any likelihood of my doing so. We are simple rustics."

"Oh, no, ma'am, I cannot concede that is so, and it is entirely possible that you will marry into Society."

"You must have windmills in your head to think so."

"I should not tease you. It is unforgivable. You are far too worthy for most of those in the *haut ton*."

"I find your reasoning incomprehensible, sir." A moment later she eyed him curiously. "You have asked on several occasions if strangers have been seen in the neighbourhood. Is it possible, Mr Jardine, that you are a fugitive from the law?"

At her suggestion he at first looked astonished and then he threw back his head and laughed heartily. Outraged, she went on, "Mayhap Sir George, who is our local magistrate, should be informed of your description."

At this threat he immediately became recalcitrant. "If I beg you not to do so you will only believe it to be true."

"Is it, Mr Jardine?"

She eyed him resolutely and he was not abashed. "If you truly believe it to be so you are an uncommonly brave woman to harbour me in your house and wander around the countryside in my company."

Her cheeks became warm, for he had made her feel foolish which was no doubt his intention. "I do not feel to be in any danger from you, sir, but I am highly suspicious. You cannot blame it in me, for you have been mightily secretive."

"Only because I hesitated to outrage your sensibilities with the truth, ma'am, but now I can see it was unfair of me and you are no vapourish female like to be shocked by the antics of this scapegrace.''

They had stopped walking and faced each other. He looked away from her again. ''I am lately resigned from my commission in the army for family reasons which, in truth, bear little relation to my . . . accident. Ever foolish I became enamoured of a certain lady whose charms proved irresistible to me.'' He paused, apparently to gauge her reaction.

''What has that to do with your . . . misfortune?'' she asked.

''Everything. Her husband arrived home unexpectedly and found her in my embrace. I was obliged to make a hasty exit despite the foul weather. It was the husband and his lackey who pursued and attacked me.''

Davinia turned away from him, striving not to let her distaste be too apparent. ''The episode does not reflect well upon you,'' she murmured at last, well aware of the shocking behaviour of some so-called gentlemen. It was invariably far worse than that of their low-born counterparts.

''Have you no word of condemnation for those who attacked me?''

''I condemn you all.''

''Are you not relieved I am no escaped felon?'' Again he looked amused.

''You evidently regard me as an ignorant chaw-bacon, Mr Jardine, unaware of the ways of the world.''

At the accusation he appeared shocked. ''Nothing could be more incorrect, my dear Miss Winterton.''

Ahead of them stood a building which was no more than a hovel. ''Is this our destination?'' he asked in surprise when she began to move towards it.

His close proximity was beginning to annoy her and she felt a desperate urge to put distance between them. Before she could reply to him an old crone came out of the building and watched them approach, her arms akimbo.

"I thought you would at least introduce me to the local gentry," he teased. "Even though you have a low opinion of me this is outside of enough."

Hiding her amusement Davinia retorted, "My errand is an urgent one and you did wish to accompany me." Her irritation never seemed to last long however much he provoked her.

"Miss Endeacott," Davinia called when they were close enough. "I have brought you some cheese and some ham."

Without a word of gratitude the woman took the basket and cast Rupert Jardine a sly glance. "I knew a stranger approached."

"You are very astute," he told her.

"Don't know what that is," the woman replied, throwing back her head.

"Are you a gypsy?" he asked then, with more respect and interest.

"Aye."

"Then mayhap you have knowledge of my horse which has been missing for several days?"

The woman laughed. "You'll not see it no more. Jud Pointer found it. Sold it by now I shouldn't wonder."

Rupert Jardine ran a hand through his fair curls. "It is as I feared. I shall be obliged to hire a post-chaise, but I suppose it is just as well. The journey will be slower but mayhap more sure."

"Do you still fear pursuit?" Davinia asked in a low voice.

It was, however, Hannah Endeacott who replied. "They've gone. Won't come back. Believe you dead, they do."

For the first time Rupert Jardine looked startled and it was odd to see him so taken aback. "As you can see, Miss Endeacott," Davinia said, a mite breathlessly a moment later, "Mr Jardine is recovered, thanks to your poultice."

The woman looked not the least gratified by the praise. "You should never have doubted it."

"I wish you could do such wonders for Papa."

"Oh, 'e's past prayin' for, and had 'is notice to quit."

Davinia's eyes filled with tears. "Oh, I beg of you do not say so!"

"Can say no more'n the truth."

"You are exceeding blunt, ma'am," Rupert Jardine said, exhibiting extreme distaste.

Hannah Endeacott cast him a malicious look. "More'n can be said of you, fine sir. It'd be a buffle-head who'd believe all your moonshine. Saw it all I did—the blood in the snow, and I knew you'd snuff it without my help."

A strange look came into his eyes then, something Davinia had not seen before, nor could she understand it. "What else did you see, old woman?" he demanded, his tongue silken no more.

"The blood on the snow. The men who wanted you dead." She turned to Davinia then. "Let me read your palm, miss."

Davinia shrank away, laughing uncomfortably. "No, no, Miss Endeacott, do not trouble, I pray."

"No trouble, miss. You've been kind to old Hannah, now let Hannah see what's in store for you."

Rupert Jardine was leaning indolently against the wall of the hovel eyeing them both with what seemed to be contempt. "Why shrink away, Miss Winterton? Do not all young ladies wish to see what is in the future for them? A handsome buck, perchance?"

Davinia flushed. "The ladies of your acquaintance evidently have windmills in their heads. I am not so foolish."

Nevertheless Hannah Endeacott took her hand and turned it palm upwards. After a moment she said, "There is a great sadness in your life, m'dear, but you will endure it and be triumphant."

"How well she assesses your character," the young man scoffed.

Undeterred by his sarcasm the old crone continued, tracing an imaginary line along Davinia's palm. "I see great love, and many riches after the danger has passed."

Davinia laughed uncomfortably. "Danger, Miss Endeacott?"

"I see danger and death."

"What a Banbury Tale!" cried Rupert Jardine and the old woman cast him a malevolent look before returning her attention to Davinia's palm.

"There's a fine house with iron gates, an eagle upon them. Yes, I see it clearly after the danger has passed. The house has turrets and grey stones, but there is happiness there; laughter and children."

She let Davinia's hand go at last and the young woman laughed uneasily. "That sounds wonderful, Miss Endeacott."

"You will not come by them easily, so be warned."

"I wonder where the house can be."

She stole a glance at Rupert Jardine and discovered that his mocking stance had gone. He had become pale and had walked away a few paces, evidently discomforted. Davinia wondered if he had overtaxed his strength after all.

The old crone looked triumphant. "It'll all come to pass; you'll see. But watch for the danger."

"Miss Winterton would be better occupied avoiding you, old woman," Rupert Jardine told her.

"You scorn old Hannah, but she sees it all. Let me show you, fine sir. Let me read yer palm."

"No, I thank you," he snapped.

Hannah Endeacott shrugged. "I don't need to. I can *see*. You've got a false heart and you're in great danger. You'd better heed my words."

He was walking briskly away. Davinia bade Hannah Endeacott a breathless "Good day," and hurried after him.

"She is outrageous, is she not? I cannot conceive what she may mean by all her babbling."

" 'Tis plain her attic is to let. Not all lunatics are confined to Bedlam."

"Shall you not heed her warning of danger?"

He cast her a smile, his ill-humour gone. "Shall you believe her vision of the future for you?"

"She knows I have suffered great sadness, but as for the rest . . . It is evident she is fanciful."

"It is also evident she witnessed what happened to me, or saw me being carried to your cottage. I fear there is no magic about it, but the way she attempted to frighten you is faint gratitude indeed."

"It is merely her manner which offends. It is always so, but I vouch her poultice really did cool your fever."

"Believe what you will, Miss Winterton. I prefer to put more credence upon your skilful nursing."

She cast him a coy glance, relieved he was no longer angry. "A little of both, perchance?"

"You have a generous heart, Miss Winterton."

"Do you have a false one, Mr Jardine?"

He smiled again and his eyes twinkled. "It would be a foolish man who admitted to such a fault."

"And a foolhardy woman who expected it of you." Davinia's brow furrowed. "Hannah has lived all her life around these parts; I wonder where she has seen a grey stone house with turrets."

He looked troubled again. "Hindlesham Park?"

"No, it is not that. Hindlesham Park is of red brick, built after the Italian style, not at all as she described."

"There will be a logical explanation, I vow. Females are for ever reading Gothic novels. It is clear her pleasures are of a similar nature and the house she describes is a part of a novel she has read."

"That cannot possibly be, for Hannah cannot read or write."

He looked suddenly brighter. "Then we must conclude she is correct. Providing you are able to brave the danger she warned you of, you have a good deal to look forward to, Miss Winterton."

For a long moment she looked at him in astonishment and then, when he began to laugh, Davinia did, too.

The sky was leaden, threatening a further fall of snow. Davinia's heart felt heavy, too, as she gazed out at the postchaise from the front parlour window.

Rupert Jardine was taking his farewell from her father, a scene she found she had no wish to witness. Suddenly a sound in the doorway made her turn around. He was wearing his caped driving coat and staring at her balefully. His manner was so different to normal, always mocking, a jest for ever on his lips.

"I must go now if I am to reach London tomorrow."

Davinia swallowed the lump that had seemed to fill her throat. "The weather is still inclement. There is a further chance of snow. Are you cer . . ."

"I must be in London on the morrow," he said gently. "There are those who will wonder what has become of me."

Davinia smiled then. "Of course. You must not delay."

"Mr Winterton seems in better health of late."

"Since my brother's death his health has deteriorated, but I know he has enjoyed your company, Mr Jardine. Your presence has cheered him greatly."

He peered at her, inclining his head a little. "And you, Miss Winterton? Does the same apply to you?"

She averted her eyes and replied in a voice no louder than a whisper, "You must know it is so."

"Thanking you seems so inadequate . . ."

"You must not," she answered quickly.

He smiled crookedly. "Then I shall not attempt to do so,

but before I leave I would like you to accept a token of my regard.''

He walked across the room and pressed something into her hands. Davinia looked down at a beautiful gold locket on a long chain.

Immediately she began to protest. ''Oh no, I cannot pos—''

He pressed her fingers around it. ''Please, Miss Winterton. It belonged to my mother and I know she would want you to have it.''

''I scarce know what to say.''

''Just accept it.''

''But it must be very valuable.''

''Not more than my life, for which I shall ever be grateful.'' She looked up at him then, tears trembling on her lashes. ''Wear it always and think of me often.''

''Oh, Mr Jardine . . .''

''I shall never forget you.''

He raised her hand to his lips and then suddenly he placed his hands on her shoulders and kissed her lightly on the lips. Shocked by the suddenness of the gesture she closed her eyes and when she opened them again he had gone. She hurried back to the window in time to see him climb into the post-chaise. He glanced at her as the postillion closed the door, but he neither waved nor indicated he had seen her.

Davinia stood at the window until the post-chaise was no longer to be seen and then she turned away, vainly attempting to stem a tide of tears. Only moments later the sound of hoofbeats sent her hurrying back to the window, this time to see Sir George Hindlesham riding up the drive.

Hastily she brushed away her tears and went to greet him when a pale-faced Molly admitted him to the cottage and took his hat, riding whip and gloves. One glance at her maid told Davinia that the girl had been crying, too.

"Sir George, it is good of you to call," Davinia greeted him breathlessly, still discomposed and in truth wishing only to be alone with her thoughts.

The young man glanced around curiously. "I wished to ascertain you all fared well. I trust you are in good health."

"Yes, indeed. How good of you to ask. Even Papa appears to be in good heart."

"And your guest?" He was looking at her curiously. "How does he do?"

Davinia was forced to look away. "He is fully recovered and has only just left for London. Had you arrived a little sooner you would have been able to meet him."

"What a pity I have missed the opportunity. I'd hoped to make his acquaintance."

"And he yours," she assured him, although she was not at all certain Rupert Jardine would have welcomed the opportunity.

"So it is not like we shall see him again."

She felt desolate. "No . . ."

"It was a queer episode, do you not agree, Miss Winterton?"

"It seemed perfectly straightforward to me. Accidents do frequently occur to all manner of people."

"Falling from a horse is more like to break one's neck as injure the head, especially when cushioned by a heavy fall of snow. Moreover on that very night two strangers put up at *The Bull*."

"What is that to Mr Jardine?" she asked heatedly, for some reason ready to defend him. A man could not be condemned for dallying with a married woman. So many bucks behaved in a far worse fashion.

Sir George shrugged. "I cannot say. Mayhap there is no connection whatsoever. I had hoped you might know the truth of the matter." Davinia turned away from him as he asked, "Did you not find him a quiz?"

"Not at all, Sir George." She moved further away from him, surreptitiously transferring the locket to her pocket. "I trust Lady Hindlesham is in good heart." To her relief he was easily diverted from the uncomfortable subject of Rupert Jardine.

"Never better. We are travelling to London next week to attend Miss Durrant's come out ball," he added with obvious discomfort and he could no longer meet Davinia's steady gaze.

"You will be gone some considerable time."

"It is very like we shall and I would wish to pay my respects to Mr Winterton before I go."

"He will be delighted to receive you, Sir George. Mayhap you will go along to the sitting room where I shall join you in a minute or two."

When he had gone Davinia eagerly took out the locket and examined it again, more closely this time. Her fingers traced the design of oak leaves etched into it and soon located the catch. On the lightest touch it sprung open to reveal a lock of golden hair, possibly the first cut from his head as a child. She smiled at the thought that he had once been young and innocent but when she heard Sir George's voice she closed the locket and put it away again, hurrying into the hall.

The young man was coming towards her and she immediately exclaimed, "What is amiss?"

"Mr Winterton," he gasped, his face white. "He is ill. You must come immediately."

Davinia felt the colour drain from her cheeks. "Yes, I shall, but first I must send Molly for Dr Brooke."

"No, no. Allow me to go in her stead. My horse is a swift one and it will be quicker. I shall fetch him here myself."

Snatching up his hat, riding whip and gloves he rushed out of the cottage just as Davinia ran into the sitting room to find her father, pale and gasping for breath in his chair. When she reached his side he grasped her hand, unable to speak, and as she stared at him in helpless horror a terrible fear gripped her heart, for she had never seen him so ill before.

PART TWO

Interlude

FIVE

Kirkland Manor had long since ceased to be a manor house in the traditional sense. For one thing, there was no longer a squire in residence. Through successive aristocratic elevations, the squires had gone from baronet to earl, and the present incumbent, Lord Kirkland, was the third of the line. As their elevation took place, so the original manor expanded to become a great mansion which better befitted their station, although parts of its Tudor beginnings remained amidst the more modern Georgian splendour.

The Manor now looked out over uninterrupted views of rolling countryside. On her marriage, the countess had embarked upon a renovation programme which included all the gardens, having them remade in the current vogue for naturalness and simplicity. Beyond the lawns and flower beds, where peacocks strutted with supreme arrogance, there now stood a lake stocked with fish for which the frequent guests to Kirkland Manor could angle and be certain of their catch. Beyond the lake, in the park, deer roamed freely, and growing in the new orangery were grapes and pineapples, where parrakeets brought from the Indies screeched as they flew from branch to branch to the amusement of all those who watched them.

The Manor, having been something of a ramshackle place before the advent of Evelina Kirkland, was now fit to receive the most elevated people in the land, and it often did so.

On this particularly pleasant summer day, the rooms echoed with the sound of hurrying feet. Maidservants bearing flowers and bowls of fruit bumped into each other leaving or entering rooms. Other servants were dusting and sweeping with a vengeance whilst in the pantry the hundreds of pieces of silver which would be used to serve gargantuan banquets were being polished. Liveried footmen went about their own tasks with a semblance of dignity whilst Lady Kirkland herself was ensconced in her boudoir with her maid.

When the last auburn curl was tucked into place the countess finally seemed satisfied. "You have done very well, Mira."

The maid looked gratified, but then less so as Davinia Winterton, her mistress's new paid companion, came into the room. The maid cast the girl a cool look as she removed Lady Kirkland's covering robe to reveal a gown of pale green muslin of the very latest mode.

"Well, Davinia, will I do?" Lady Kirkland asked as she fastened a necklace of pearls around her white throat.

"You look quite ravishing, my lady," she replied in all truthfulness.

The woman appeared to be delighted. "You are a sweet child." She walked out of her dressing room and back into the bedchamber, leaving her maid to tidy up. The countess suddenly put one hand to her head. "Such a to-do. I feel an attack of the vapours coming on."

Davinia cast her an amused look. "That would be quite unlike you, my lady."

"Indeed. I have never been the type of person to swoon, but there is always a first time, I feel. Mrs Fairchild is a good enough housekeeper, but Davinia, dear, I would deem it a great favour if you would check all the guests' rooms . . ."

"I have already done so, my lady. Discreetly, of course. I

would not wish to offend Mrs Fairchild. Everything is in order and just as you wished.''

Lady Kirkland looked astonished. ''Are there only *red* roses in Lady Grindle's room? No flowers at all in Lord Fontanel's, for they only make him sneeze? He is most particular on that score. And,'' she added with a smile, ''a fresh pineapple in Lord Ravelston's? He is most partial, I recall.''

''Everything is exactly as you ordered, my lady.''

The countess relaxed a little then. ''Whatever did I do without you?''

''You contrived handsomely before my arrival,'' Davinia pointed out although she felt gratified all the same.

It had been more than six months since the death of John Winterton. Although he had ailed for so long his death had nevertheless come as a bitter blow to his daughter. Their acquaintances in the neighbourhood had been more than kind in her bereavement, but after it was over Davinia was faced with the unpleasant realisation that she was alone in the world and without means. Moreover the cottage she had always known as home had been that only during her father's lifetime. Sir George and Lady Hindlesham had assured her she could remain for as long as she wished, but knowing she must at some time leave, Davinia resolved to do so at the first opportunity, for no amount of delay could avert the final wrench.

It was Lady Hindlesham herself who found the solution. An acquaintance of hers had recently lost a dear sister and was in need of a companion. Davinia did not relish the thought of becoming a paid companion but as she was qualified to be nothing else knew she had no choice in the matter, and Lady Hindlesham did paint a rosy picture.

''Evelina Kirkland is the most delightful creature you are ever like to meet,'' she had enthused. ''All amiability and condescension, I assure you. She was a great beauty in her youth, although she was foolish enough to make a disastrous marriage. Hugo Moncrieff was in the worst way of being a scapegrace, for ever in scrapes and dun territory. Fortunately he had the consideration to die shortly afterwards and now dear Evelina is married to Kirkland. He is a contemporary of my own dear Will, years older than Evelina, but he adores her and can refuse her nothing. The marriage is quite successful I believe. I am persuaded you will settle at Kirkland Manor very nicely.''

And so Davinia reluctantly set about disposing of most of her father's vast collection of books, keeping a few precious ones for her own use and took her leave of Hindlesham and all she knew there. With her own few belongings she set out for Kirkland Manor, her heart filled with foreboding, for she had often heard tell of the miserable existence of those obliged to become paid companions, but it transpired that Lady Hindlesham was not wrong. Evelina Kirkland was as delightful as she had been described. All who knew her evidently adored her and she welcomed Davinia warmly. Soon Davinia settled into her home to pander to the relatively undemanding life as the countess's companion.

Lady Kirkland looked across the room to where a bowl of flowers was set on a table in the corner. ''None of the maids can arrange flowers as you do. No one could be as attentive and as kind as you, and as for my own daughter . . . well, the less I say about Lizzie the better. Her behaviour is outside of enough these days.''

''It is a delight to serve you, my lady. All the servants say so, too.''

Lady Kirkland chuckled with delight, asking, ''How is Kirkland today? Have you seen him this morning?''

''No, ma'am, I believe he . . .''

The countess put one hand up to prevent Davinia saying more. ''Yes, I know. He was foxed before ten o'clock last night. His head will ache abominably this morning and he will be most reluctant to show his face before noon. Well, as long as he is able to greet our guests when they arrive I shall not scold him.''

"Oh, I am persuaded he will."

Lady Kirkland looked less certain but then she put one hand to her head. "My sensibilities are quite overset, Davinia. Guests have been welcomed here ever since I married Kirkland, but this time we are actually hosting a *government* minister."

"You have no cause for alarm on that score, Lady Kirkland," Davinia assured her. "You are well-acquainted with Lord and Lady Castlereagh, are you not?"

"Dear Emily, certainly, but not so much the viscount. He is so busy. He rarely takes his leisure, so I am not so well-acquainted with him. With the war still continuing unabated we are singularly honoured by his presence."

"Most certainly but surely no more than when the Duke stayed here. A royal duke no less."

"Yes, yes, you are quite correct. Fitz is much more important, but all the same I am in a fidge lest something goes wrong during Castlereagh's stay."

"Nothing possibly can, my lady," Davinia told her in a soothing tone. "Do not get into a pucker over this, I beg of you. Would you wish me to rub your forehead with cologne, my lady?"

"Later I shall no doubt beg for you to so, but now I believe I shall contrive, my dear. I would prefer you to help me to decide what gowns to wear in the next few days."

As Lady Kirkland walked towards the press Davinia replied, "Every one you possess is exquisite, my lady."

"You must learn to be discerning, Davinia."

"You can always guide me, my lady."

"Always? I think not, my dear. One day you will capture the heart of some pleasant young man and I shall be obliged to find a less agreeable companion."

"I shouldn't think so, Lady Kirkland. Even young men

without means have a reluctance to pay court to penniless females and I cannot find it in my heart to blame them.''

''My dear, before Kirkland married me I was as poor as a church rat. Moncrieff made certain of that.''

Davinia forbore to remind her that she was an accepted member of the *ton* and also very beautiful which made all the difference in the world.

As the day progressed the liveried footmen took on the appearance of worker ants, for as soon as the first guests began to arrive they started to bear chests and portmanteaux in great numbers to the various appointed bedchambers. The house steward added to the general mêlée by harrying those servants under him, whilst Mrs Fairchild, the housekeeper, her keys clanking at her belt, scolded the maids unmercifully.

There was no respite for any of them. No sooner had the first carriage arrived than another followed in quick succession. Davinia was familiar with the names on the guest list, but now she would be obliged to attach faces to titles which were already known to her. That task took on the semblance of a game as she watched the arrivals from the first landing. Lord and Lady Kirkland, he looking perfectly sober, hurried to the hall to greet their guests as each carriage approached. The countess was an accomplished hostess, but Davinia was well aware, on this occasion, she was nervous of having Lord Castlereagh as a guest. It was well known that he rarely took his place in Society, which in truth meant indulging in all its diversions. The war with France kept him constantly occupied so that his acceptance was something of a triumph for Lady Kirkland.

As Davinia peered over the bannister at the latest arrivals she became aware of a presence nearby. Before she looked around she knew who it must be—Lizzie Moncrieff. The countess had only one child, from her early disastrous marriage, a girl of some seventeen years. How someone as beautiful as Lady Kirkland could have produced such a plain child Davinia was at a loss to explain, but it was so. Lizzie with her straw colour hair and thin body bore little resemblance to her beautiful mother or, if gossip was to be believed, her late, dashing father. Her only redeeming feature was a pair of deep green eyes which often sparkled with either malice or mischief, and frequently with a mixture of both. It seemed evident that many of the spotty and bloodless youths invited to Kirkland Manor were there for Lizzie's sake even though her come-out was some months away.

"So the arrivals have begun," the girl said in a flat voice as she joined Davinia by the landing.

"Lord and Lady Grindle are already here, and Mr Monkswood, who is quite the bang-up blade, has just arrived." Davinia cast her a curious glance. "Should you not be at Lord and Lady Kirkland's side?"

Lizzie shrugged her thin shoulders. "We shall all have a surfeit of them before many days have passed, and in any event they are all Mama's cronies or those of Lord Kirkland."

"Not all. Mr Livesey is not."

"He is certainly not one of mine!" The girl leaned over the bannister rail. "Oh, just look, Miss Winterton; that is Lord Fontanel," she pointed out with a giggle. "Oh, what a cake he has made of himself."

He was a man who dressed in the extreme style of the dandies, something the girl despised if her tone was anything by which to judge. The points of his shirt collar were so high it was hard to believe he could see anything at all, let alone move his head.

"I was wondering who he might be," Davinia murmured. "I am obliged to you for the information."

"He is a great bore. Indeed, they all are."

Davinia laughed softly. "Oh, I am persuaded that cannot

be so, Miss Moncrieff. Your Mama would not countenance such people about her."

"Well, mayhap not all of them are tedious. Lady Grindle is quite pleasant, I own, and a beauty. She is always attentive to me." Her plain, thin features suddenly came alive. "And there is Lord Ravelston, of course."

Davinia recognised the name from the guest list although she had not met him before. "You like him, too?" she asked with interest, for it was unusual enough to discover this girl enlivened by anyone or anything.

"*Everyone* likes Ravel. He's always playing old Harry, and is the greatest fun, although," she lowered her voice, "he's a terrible rake. I am not supposed to know, but he is for ever in a scrape. Whenever he is staying here, the maids fight for the privilege of putting a brick in his bed or making up his fire. Mrs Asket *times* how long they are gone from the kitchen."

Davinia laughed. "Miss Moncrieff, you are roasting me!"

The girl's eyes grew wide. "I assure you I am not. You will see for yourself during his stay here, and I declare that even you, Miss Winterton, will fall prey to his charms."

Again Davinia laughed at the girl's naïveté. "If he is as you say, such weakness is bound to be dangerous and I would not be so foolish. Moreover, if you harbour a partiality for such a man you are like to find difficulty choosing a suitable husband who exhibits more sobriety."

Her face crinkled into an expression of disgust. "Most certainly a husband Mama would approve of and I would hate to marry some like Dick Cherry or Samuel Livesey, although they are being talked about as suitors."

"They seemed to be perfectly nice young men."

Her face appeared to be permanently twisted into a grimace of distaste. "Tush! Lord Kirkland will dangle my portion in front of them and it is certain they will reach for it

like fish about to be caught on a hook. Ravelston would not
seek a fortune.''

"Well, perchance your charm and youth will bring him
up to scratch after your debut.''

Lizzie laughed, a mite coyly. "That is certainly not my
aim for he is much too old for me.''

"Age is no barrier. Your own mama is an example of
that. She and Lord Kirkland are sublimely happy.''

Lizzie Moncrieff's mind, however, was not on her
mother and step-father. "Ravelston always declared himself
a bachelor for life, but I am given to understand he has recently become betrothed. Well, I for one do not envy any
wife of his. She will be well advised to make certain every
female servant is a harridan of at least five and seventy.
Even so he is not to be trusted. Oh, here is Lord and Lady
Castlereagh!''

Davinia's mind was immediately diverted as Lizzie
added, "How pale he looks and how handsome.''

To Davinia's mind the viscount looked too frail to have
such a huge burden thrust upon him. He was, however,
quite handsome and his wife a pretty woman, too. It was
said they were exceedingly content together, something
comparatively rare within the circles of the *haut ton*.

"Do you think the country is safe whilst he is here?'' Lizzie asked in a harsh whisper as Davinia watched the couple
being welcomed by their host and hostess.

Davinia cast her an amused look. "I am quite persuaded it
is. Lord Castlereagh is not single-handedly holding back the
armies of Buonaparte.''

"Mayhap Boney will decide to invade England whilst
Lord Castlereagh is here with us!''

"How will Boney know?''

Lizzie's eyes grew wide as she glanced around. "Spies
are *everywhere*, Miss Winterton. Did you not know that?
Boney knows everything.''

Davinia was still looking amused when Lizzie glanced

out of the oriel window. Her demeanour immediately changed to one of delight. "He's here. Ravel's curricle has just arrived; it's quite splendid. It must be new. I must go and greet him."

As she rushed towards the stairs Davinia asked mischievously, "Should you show partiality towards one particular guest?"

"Ravel and I are old friends," the girl replied, feigning sophistication. "He was once one of Mama's lovers."

Davinia strove hard to hide her own amusement, but was all at once anxious to see the one man Lizzie held in high esteem. However, as he came striding into the hall to Lady Kirkland's loud exclamations of greeting, Davinia's smile faded. The Marquis of Ravelston was as handsome as Davinia had expected from Lizzie's description of him. He wore a multi-caped driving coat which he flung off with a flourish and a high-crowned beaver hat which he tossed towards one of the unprepared lackeys, laughing as the man almost fell to his knees in an effort to catch it. Beneath the riding coat he wore a brown broadcloth coat of excellent cut and wrinkle free breeches. His pure linen shirt, adorned by a modicum of Flanders's lace, was finished by an immaculate folded neckcloth adorned by a diamond pin, and his Hessian boots bore an excellent shine which was undimmed by the dust of the journey.

As she looked down at the familiar figure she had thought never to see again Davinia understand all too well Lizzie Moncrieff's admiration. He was just as she recalled. He was as tall, as fair and as arrogant as she remembered, only Davinia had known him as Rupert Jardine, not the Marquis of Ravelston.

"Miss Moncrieff," Davinia said in a harsh whisper which caused the girl to turn on her heel. "Is *that* Lord Ravelston?"

"The fifth marquis," she answered pertly. "Is he not

quite the handsomest man you have ever clapped eyes upon?''

Davinia could not answer. Her mouth had become dry, her thoughts bewildered. She watched Lizzie skipping down the steps towards him, feeling oddly afraid.

He greeted the girl warmly, saying in a familiar voice which carried well, ''I see you are still the hoydon, Lizzie.''

''I despair of ever turning her into a lady,'' her mother complained.

''Ravel does not like demure ladies,'' Lizzie pointed out, looking pert. Her thin face was, for once, animated.

''How well this child knows me!'' he retorted.

''I am not a child and if you say I am I shall hate you!'' Lizzie cried.

Davinia waited to hear no more. She turned on her heel, walking quickly towards her room, knowing that now her guests were arriving Lady Kirkland would not need her for the time being and she could be alone to recover from the shock.

SIX

False heart. Hannah Endeacott's voice echoed in Davinia's mind. The old woman had been correct about him after all. He had lied about his name and heaven knew what else. A rake, Lizzie had called him. That was undoubtedly true also. By his own admission he was a scapegrace. Davinia wondered why she was so surprised. Those few days in his company showed her nothing of his true nature.

The locket was lying in her hand as she gazed down at it, her heart heavy. *It belonged to my mother*, he had said. As her fingers closed over it, Davinia doubted even that was true. More likely he had won it in some game of faro or hazard.

Ever since he had given it to her she had kept it with her, believing it to be a genuine gift from his heart. False heart. Now Davinia wrapped it in a handkerchief and dropped it in a drawer which she closed with a firm finality. It was an abject lesson and one she had learned well; never to believe the words of an obvious tonguepad.

She heard a clock chime the hour. She had never felt less like dining and knew all at once she could not face Lady Kirkland's guests with equanimity that evening. Since becoming the countess's companion Davinia had done all that was asked of her, and gladly. On this occasion she felt no guilt at pleading a headache, for the dull throbbing in her temples had become more insistent as the day progressed, and in any event with the house filled with guests she would not be missed.

Although Lady Kirkland was fully engaged entertaining her guests she was kind enough to send her personal maid with a dose of laudanum which Davinia was glad to swallow. Mercifully, after that, she slept and was aware of nothing more until the next morning when she awoke at an unusually late hour.

Realising she could not feign illness indefinitely without being discovered a fraud she stoically went about choosing a suitable gown. Her press was packed with beautiful clothes suitable for all occasions, due to the generosity of Lady Kirkland. As a matter of course the countess discarded all her gowns after one season and there had been a great many of them when Davinia had arrived at the Manor with her one cloakbag. Lady Kirkland was, however, considerably plumper than Davinia but a few stitches soon adapted all the gowns to perfection.

When Davinia initially protested at being given so many garments the countess had declared, "I cannot tolerate a dowd in my household, and in any event I am obliged to make room in my press for this Season's new gowns," thus silencing all Davinia's misgivings.

The day had dawned a fine one again so she chose a gown of sprigged muslin which was high-waisted with a pale blue sash and tiny puff sleeves. Pale blue satin slippers matched it and because Davinia possessed no jewellery of her own she had fashioned a band of matching velvet to go around her throat. After the reign of terror in France it had been the fashion to wear red ribbons around the throat to show sympathy for those who went to the guillotine. That fashion had found no favour with Davinia, however.

Several people were already breakfasting when she went downstairs, rather hesitantly. After a quick glance around the table she was able to sigh with relief, for Lord Ravelston was not present. Nor were the Castlereaghs. Many of the gentlemen were slow to rise on a morning after an evening partaking of their host's excellent wine.

Lady Kirkland greeted Davinia warmly the moment she entered the room. "My dear, are you recovered from your indisposition?"

"Yes, I thank you, my lady."

"Then do sit down and join us. You still look rather peaked, I fear. I do trust you're not sickening for a chill. It would be most inopportune for I declare the next few days will be most diverting."

"I assure you I am not," Davinia told her as she took her place at the table. "You must tell me what you wish me to do for you today."

"After breakfast you may retrieve my shawl from the summer house where I was foolish enough to leave it yesterday."

Glad of having a task to perform Davinia replied, "I shall certainly do so immediately after breakfast, my lady."

The countess continued her conversation with a lady Davinia knew to be Mrs Henley as Lizzie confided, "You missed a wonderful evening. After dinner we moved back the furniture, rolled up the carpets and danced."

"I am truly sorry to have missed it."

"Well, it isn't like that you would have been asked to stand up in any event," the girl went on bluntly.

"I should have enjoyed watching," Davinia replied, not at all put out.

"I should not like that at all." The girl cast Davinia a curious look. "Does it not grieve you to have to seek employment, Miss Winterton?"

Davinia smiled. "For a female in my situation there is precious little choice, and indeed I could not wish for a more congenial position."

"However congenial I should dislike it heartily."

"Then it is fortunate you will never have to seek employment. You have ahead of you marriage and your own establishment.''

"Oh, yes, indeed," the girl replied, her mouth full of food. "Lord Kirkland is as rich as Croesus and is providing me with a handsome portion. No doubt he believes he will be rid of me the quicker."

She giggled and then the door opened. Lizzie Moncrieff looked up, her eyes growing bright. "Good morning to you, Ravel. Do come and sit by me."

Davinia, having her back towards the door, stiffened and sitting bolt upright she reached for a slice of bread and butter.

"It is time you learned to express respect, my girl," her mother admonished. "Ravel indeed."

"All Lord Ravelston's cronies call him that."

"You are not numbered amongst them."

"I do beg your pardon, Lord Ravelston," the girl said with mock regret, eyeing him mischievously all the while.

"Accepted," he retorted, going immediately to his hostess and raising her hand to his lips. "How do you contrive to look so ravishing at such an early hour, Lady Kirkland?"

"It is almost ten-thirty and save your moonshine for those naïve enough to believe it. Do have some breakfast, for you are one of the few gentlemen resident here who can crack as many bottles as any other and yet contrive to be in high feather the following morning."

"Now who is talking moonshine?" he teased. It was then that he caught sight of Davinia whose eyes were downcast. After a moment he drew out a chair and sat down. "I thought I had met all your guests," he said in a quiet tone, unlike his more usual exuberant one.

"You have, Ravelston, I assure you," the countess replied and then realising to whom he referred went on, "Miss Winterton—Davinia—is engaged as my companion, and has been for more than six months. Last night she had the headache. As you haven't visited us for some considerable time you cannot have met her."

"You are quite incorrect, Lady Kirkland, Miss Winterton and I have met on another occasion."

At this admission Davinia did look up. He was gazing at her sombrely but it was the first time Davinia had seen the countess at a loss for words.

"Where on earth . . . ? Oh yes, indeed. For a moment I was quite taken aback but no doubt it was at Lady Hindlesham's."

Neither Davinia nor the marquis contradicted her. In fact Davinia scarce knew what to say. He helped himself to substantial helpings of food before he asked, "How is Mr Winterton keeping? I recall he was in the way of being an invalid."

"Papa died just after . . . not long before I came here."

He stopped eating and his eyes filled with genuine pain. "I am truly sorry, Miss Winterton. I should have realised . . . You have my deepest sympathy. It was a great privilege to have met him."

For once she felt he was being genuine and truthful and she guessed that was a rare enough occurrence. Lady Kirkland was gazing at him curiously, but her daughter was making no attempt to hide her displeasure.

"Miss Winterton, you have been less than frank with me. You did not tell me you had met Lord Ravelston before today."

"From the brief glance I had of him when he arrived I was not certain of his lordship's identity."

At that statement Lizzie erupted into sudden and unexpected laughter. "Only see, Ravel, not every female has your image indelibly etched into her mind and heart."

He turned to smile at the girl. " 'Tis amazing, I own, Lizzie, but like Boney I cannot win every encounter."

Davinia pushed back her chair and murmured her excuses. "I shall fetch your shawl immediately, my lady."

"Oh, do not trouble, my dear. I shall not require it for a while and I beg of you do not over exert yourself, for I shall not be in need of your services during the house party."

As Davinia went towards the door she had the feeling the marquis was watching her, and it was a disconcerting experience. One thing she was quite certain about—he exhibited no pleasure at seeing her.

As she left the dining room a young woman was about to enter. She cast Davinia a haughty look as she passed without speaking, and Davinia thought her quite beautiful with pale cheeks, fair curls and eyes the colour of sapphires.

Davinia fetched her chip-straw bonnet and paisley shawl and slipped out of the house by a side-entrance. Now the first encounter was over she felt better about his presence, for she had no cause for embarrassment in his company, although it was evident his feelings were not similar.

Several gentlemen were out in the grounds, no doubt hoping the good country air would dispel the headaches caused by imbibing too freely of Lord Kirkland's claret. Davinia bade all she encountered a bright "Good morning," but elicited no more than bad-tempered grunts from them.

The summer house, built on classical lines like a Greek temple, was on a hillock at the far side of the grounds and afforded a wonderful view of the lake where, no doubt, a fishing party would take place before the house guests left for home.

Lady Kirkland's paisley shawl was lying on a bench and Davinia folded it carefully. As she turned to leave she started with shock, seeing the marquis standing in the doorway behind her. It angered and confused her to realise he must have followed her from the house. He was leaning nonchalantly against the door, eyeing her sombrely, which caused her to feel quite discomforted once again.

Davinia wondered uneasily what to do, what to say. Meeting him in a crowded room was one thing; here alone with him quite another. After a few moments her dilemma was solved when he spoke first.

"It was a great surprise for me to see you here."

"No more than it surprised me to see you, my lord, for I did not recognise your name from the guest list. No one named Rupert Jardine was listed."

He came further into the summer house increasing her unease. "You must wonder what I was about."

"No, no," she protested. "It is of no account I assure you."

"It is to me, Miss Winterton. I did not lie to you. The name I gave you is genuine and one I have used for most of my life. The title I now bear is one inherited not long ago from my late uncle."

"Does it matter?"

"Not a great deal, I own," he replied, smiling at her, "but I wanted you to know the truth."

She smiled, too, although it cost her dear to do so. "I am obliged to you for the explanation, but it was not necessary. I would have endeavoured to help the Marquis of Ravelston as I did Rupert Jardine, or indeed had it been one of the local farmhands. Your true identity is of no account to me, I assure you."

"You relieve my mind on that score, ma'am." At that point in their conversation she would have gone past him but he placed himself foursquare in her way. "I also wish to thank you for not revealing the true circumstances of our previous meeting to all those present today. It might well have proved embarrassing if you had."

She gasped, feeling exasperated now. "Lord Ravelston, I am no tattle-basket even if anyone should consider my words worth listening to, but I cannot understand your reticence in so small a matter. Everyone present is under no illusions as to your behaviour, and would, in no way, be surprised."

He smiled engagingly. "I had no notion I was so famous."

"As I see it, infamous would be a far better description."

"My word, how alarming that is, and you sound so disapproving, Miss Winterton. I cannot credit it in you."

Again there was the mockery in his manner which had so entranced her at Hindlesham. Now it only irritated her. "It is not for a paid companion to disapprove of one of her employer's guests."

"As I recall you were never so Friday-faced at Hindlesham."

"My circumstances have changed quite radically since then, my lord."

The mockery died at her reminder. "That is true indeed. Tell me, Miss Winterton, how did you come by this post?"

"Through Lady Hindlesham. She was kind enough to enquire of her acquaintances for a suitable post. I have cause to be greatly obliged to her."

"How true that is. The only misfortune is that Kirkland Manor is so far removed from Hindlesham, but I dare say that was as much to Lady Hindlesham's regret as yours."

When Davinia did nothing save stare down at her feet he asked, affecting a languid air, "How is Sir George? I take it he is not a guest here, too, for I cannot recall seeing him."

"Sir George, as far as I am aware, is in rude health and great spirits. He was married in the spring to the former Miss Clarinda Durrant."

Once again she made to go past him. This time he caught her by the arm and drew her back. "I am truly sorry about that, Miss Winterton."

"I cannot conceive why, Lord Ravelston. It was the occasion for great rejoicing. Pray excuse me now. I must return to the house; Lady Kirkland will be in need of me."

"I distinctly heard her say she would not be requiring your services whilst her guests were here. However, if you feel you must return, allow me to escort you back."

As they walked along one shore of the lake he said, glancing at her, "I note you do not wear the locket I gave you."

It was a question she had dreaded hearing him ask. "Indeed I do not. It would be improper for me to wear jewellery given by a stranger."

For a moment he did not reply and as she cast him a wary glance, he said, staring ahead of him, "You have a cruel tongue when you so wish, Miss Winterton."

" 'Tis better than a false heart," she could not help but retort.

They had re-entered the gardens where one or two guests cast them a curious look. Strolling along the gravel Broad Walk directly before the front elevation of the Manor were many people, amongst them the beautiful girl Davinia had admired outside the dining room that morning. She had been strolling with a rather corpulent gentleman and at the sight of them came running forward across the grass.

"Ravelston!" she cried, displaying a pronounced French accent. "I have been looking for you *everywhere*."

"Not everywhere, my dear," he contradicted, "else you would surely have found me."

His manner had changed once more. He was once again the urbane and charming buck with a quick turn of wit. Davinia found such rapid changes of manner totally bewildering.

The girl fixed Davinia with a malevolent look and the marquis said quickly, "This is Miss Winterton, Veronique, Lady Kirkland's new companion."

The young woman's eyes grew wide. "Are companions allowed to mix freely with guests in this country?"

Davinia stiffened angrily but the marquis answered, "My dear, if your countrymen had shown a similar magnanimity towards their servants the revolution would never have happened and Lord Castlereagh would not be obliged to curtail so much of his pleasure to manage the war."

"Now you are roasting me," she countered, fluttering her eyelashes in a most beguiling manner.

The corpulent man came puffing up to them, saying breathlessly, "Ravelston, I have been talking to Castlereagh about this cursed war. I told him it has gone on long enough."

"I am sure he knows that, m'sieur." The marquis then turned to Davinia, saying, "Miss Winterton, this is Le Comte du Plessy, Veronique's father."

The comte took Davinia's hand and raised it to his lips. "*Enchanté*, mademoiselle."

"Papa," the girl added, "Mademoiselle Winterton is Lady Kirkland's *companion*."

A look of surprise crossed the Frenchman's face and as soon as Davinia could, she extricated her hand, saying, "You are an *emigré*, m'sieur. How dreadful this entire business is."

"*Mais oui*," the comte agreed. "I live in hope that one day soon my daughter will be able to see her ancestral home when it is returned to me."

"No doubt you live in hope of that," Davinia murmured.

"*Certainement*. The infamous regime must be routed. Castlereagh agrees that it will be very soon."

"Papa," Veronique chided from behind her fan, "Miss Winterton does not wish to know of our misfortunes."

"A Frenchman's misfortune is also ours," the marquis told her, "as I am certain Miss Winterton will agree."

"My brother was killed at Trafalgar," she told them.

"The French have always been such good sailors and fighting men," the comte replied. "This war will not be over so soon, I fear."

"I trust you are incorrect," the marquis replied, looking slightly vexed but losing none of his aplomb.

"In any event, my home is in England now," the young Frenchwoman said, glancing at the marquis before adding, "more so now than before."

"Come, Ravelston," the comte urged, "let us leave the ladies to their tattle. Castlereagh would like to make your acquaintance."

The marquis looked less than eager to leave their company, but after a momentary hesitation bowed to them and walked away with the comte. Veronique du Plessy's eyes followed them before she turned to Davinia again, looking at her speculatively.

"You must forgive my presumption, Miss er . . . ?"

"Winterton," Davinia supplied.

The girl smiled. "I did not intend to insult you, but in France servants never ever mix with members of the household in such a familiar way."

Far from being annoyed Davinia was now amused at the girl's naïveté and was hard-put not to show it. Instead she replied demurely, "I do understand although I believe life in France is quite different now for the *haut monde*."

The barb went home which gave Davinia some comfort before Mademoiselle du Plessy asked, "Have you been acquainted with Ravelston for long, Miss Winterton?"

The girl seemed more than anxious to know. "Hardly at all," Davinia replied in all truthfulness. "We have merely met on another occasion, mam'selle."

Veronique du Plessy stole another glance at the marquis as she fluttered her fan. "In all honesty I was most reluctant to come here this week. I find such gatherings a trifle tedious and I do so long to be in London to plan my trousseau."

"You are to be married?" Davinia asked, exhibiting genuine interest.

"*Mais oui*. Ravelston and I are only recently betrothed but we are to be married very soon. Indeed, we have scarce been apart since we first met during last Season." Davinia was only just digesting this information when, fluttering her embroidered fan once again, the girl added, "If you will excuse me. I must go now and rescue him from Papa."

Davinia watched her go in dismay, her head reeling. She

scarce had time to marshal her thoughts before Lizzie Moncrieff came sidling up to her, making her start.

"Oh, Miss Moncrieff," she gasped, "you gave me a shock."

Uncaring, the girl demanded, "What do you think of her?"

"Who?" Davinia asked perversely

"Veronique du Plessy. I saw you in earnest conversation with her which is indeed a remarkable feat in itself."

"She is very beautiful."

"That is not in doubt," the girl answered irritably. "Ravel is quite a judge in such matters, but all the same she is as poor as can be. The comte escaped from France without a guinea to his name so the marquis is quite a catch for his dear daughter."

"It was you who said only yesterday he would not dangle after a fortune."

"Mama says he has scarce been absent from her side since they met. I suppose even rakes fall in love sometimes, only I wish it had not happened to be someone like Veronique du Plessy. I cannot own that they are well-suited."

"Surely Lord Ravelston is a better judge of that."

"I wonder." Suddenly the girl giggled behind her fan. "That accent—it's so false. Had you noticed?"

"Mademoiselle du Plessy is French, Miss Moncrieff."

"She left France when she was no more than a babe, so it cannot possibly be true, but no doubt Ravel finds her manner irresistible. I hadn't thought him such a chuckle-head."

Davinia glanced across to where they were all in conversation with Lord Castelreagh. Veronique du Plessy looked vexed and bored, no doubt because their attention was not at that moment fixed upon her. "Yes, no doubt he does. I must go indoors and return this shawl to Lady Kirkland's room."

"Come along with me instead and watch me annoy the fair Veronique."

Davinia's eyes grew wide. "Miss Moncrieff, you must not!"

Lizzie looked smug. "Don't get into a pucker, Miss Winterton. 'Tis easy to achieve with very little effort. I have known Ravel all my life and I only have to mention the fact for Mademoiselle du Plessy to grow vexed. Foolish chit . . . As if she can be his first love. 'Tis best to be the last."

At such a sage pronouncement Davinia could not help but laugh, watching helplessly as the girl skipped off to do her mischief.

SEVEN

As she walked along the gallery Davinia could hear the sounds of laughter emanating from the downstairs rooms. For once she was less than anxious to join the guests for dinner but knew she was bound to on this occasion.

Suddenly her step faltered as she heard what sounded like low laughter close by. Just as she was about to go on, Mira, Lady Kirkland's personal maid, appeared in the doorway of one of the rooms at the end of the gallery. When she caught sight of Davinia she covered her mouth to stifle her laughter. As the girl ran past, Davinia paused again to stare after her curiously. Then she understood better when Lord Ravelston, resplendent in his evening coat, came out of the room after her.

He, however, displayed no discomposure at being caught in an indiscretion. Davinia didn't doubt it happened often enough to be commonplace.

"Ah, Miss Winterton," he greeted her. "Allow me to escort you downstairs."

She had no choice but to concur. As they walked down the stairs together he asked, "Are you settled at Kirkland Manor?"

"Yes, indeed, my lord. Life here is most comfortable and Lord and Lady Kirkland kindness itself."

"I admire them greatly," he admitted, and then to her surprise he added in a lower tone, "That shade of blue suits you. I implore you to wear it often."

She gasped with exasperation. "Lord Ravelston, do you not ever grow weary of filling gullible females with moonshine?"

He was evidently taken aback by her sharpness. "It was not moonshine, I assure you, but the veritable truth. I am by nature an admirer of females, but if they all reacted as you do to a perfectly natural response, I should indeed grow weary of it very quickly."

Davinia then felt both foolish and embarrassed and countered, "I quite forgot to congratulate you on your recent betrothal, my lord."

He paused at the foot of the stairs to gaze at her before replying, "How kind of you. I must be the most fortunate of men."

"That is the general opinion."

"She will make an excellent wife, will she not?"

"I trust you are not soliciting *my* opinion upon that," Davinia snapped.

"Why should I not? You seem a woman of very good sense."

"If you insist that I express an opinion . . ."

"I do."

"Mademoiselle du Plessy is beautiful and charming. You could not wish for more."

He smiled faintly, almost mockingly. "No indeed. I am entirely in agreement with you, Miss Winterton. What is elegance, wit and good sense against such qualities? There, is it not pleasant to be in agreement for once?"

She cast him an exasperated look, knowing he was teasing her once more. There were few enough subjects which he would treat with any degree of seriousness, and it appeared that of his wife-to-be was not one of them. They had gravitated towards the drawing room, the doors of which had been flung open. A pair of liveried footmen stood at either side and bowed low as they approached. Having caught sight of them in the hall Mademoiselle du Plessy immediately hurried forward.

"Ravelston, where have you been?" She cast Davinia an angry look. "I have been waiting for an age."

Not at all put out by her anger he countered, "Do not scold me, my love. Miss Winterton was singing your praises and I could not bear to stop her doing so."

The girl looked immediately gratified and Davinia had to admire his silken tongue. Casting him an exasperated look she went further into the room, leaving the couple alone together.

Later Lady Kirkland said to Davinia, "Although I confess myself surprised to see you on convivial terms with Lord Ravelston, I am glad to see it is so."

Annoyed that anyone should think her so foolish she felt bound to retort, "You are mistaken, my lady. Naturally I am polite to him, as I would be to any of your guests, but I am bound to tell you that he is the kind of man I abhor."

Davinia was aware of having shocked her employer but it was true and she could not help but voice her feelings at last. Moreover, she disliked Lord Ravelston thoroughly although at the same time she was aware of the unjustness of her feelings. The marquis had never pretended to be other than a rake but at times, when they'd been at Beech Tree Cottage, she was certain she had glimpsed more, and could not forgive him for disappointing her so deeply.

"Lady Kirkland is such an accomplished hostess," Veronique du Plessy cooed later that evening. "I must observe her closely, for I, too, will have a large establishment to run when I am married."

As she spoke she bestowed a gracious smile upon Davinia who said, "It is a daunting task."

"I shall enjoy it, even rusticating will be delightful when I am with my dear Ravelston."

"Where are Lord Ravelston's estates situated?" Davinia enquired, genuinely interested in knowing.

The girl was obliged to consider carefully. "There is a large house in Town, naturally, as well as the hunting lodge at Pembury. Ravelston's main house is Brookfield in Northamptonshire. I am told the house is as large as this one. It was once a castle and most of the original walls are intact. I cannot wait until Ravelston takes me there as his bride although I do confess a slight apprehension. I am sadly inexperienced in such matters as running a large establishment. Ravelston says I must not think of it."

"I am persuaded you will contrive," Mrs. Henley told her and then, smiling coyly, "Lord Ravelston will only require you to look fetching."

Veronique du Plessy dimpled at the compliment. "So he is always telling me, ma'am."

The lengthy and delicious dinner had been over for some time although the gentlemen were still taking their port in the dining room. In the large drawing room with its pale blue upholstery and pilastered walls, the ladies gathered in small groups to converse or to sew. Most did both whilst the footmen put up card tables for those unable to resist the urge to gamble.

Veronique du Plessy clasped both hands together at her breast. "It would be so pleasant if we could dance again tonight. I enjoyed it so much last evening. Mayhap Lady Kirkland will sanction it when the gentlemen join us. Miss Winterton, you missed it last evening, but I was not obliged to sit out one set. It has always been so whenever I have attended balls or routs. I pity with all my heart those poor creatures who are obliged to sit out set after set because no man wishes for their company." As she spoke she directed an innocent smile towards Lizzie who affected not to notice. "They are best employed playing the spinet, I feel. Then it is not so evident and their humiliation is not as great. Do *you* play, Miss Winterton?"

"Not as well as I would like, mam'selle."

"I fear you are too modest. I am persuaded you must be

exceeding accomplished and have more time than most for practice. I am but a poor player myself. I have always been in so much demand by my acquaintances such pursuits have become almost impossible.''

"So many ladies exaggerate their accomplishments," Lizzie answered darkly, "Miss Winterton's modesty is a most refreshing change and her honesty is much to be admired.''

Davinia could not help but smile over her sewing and more so as Lizzie went on, "I do agree with you wholeheartedly, Mademoiselle du Plessy, over the question of being obliged to sit out sets. However, I am bound to admit I pity more those females with only windmills in their heads, those whose sole accomplishment is the ability to flirt and to dance. I fear their husbands must soon grow heartily bored with them.''

Veronique du Plessy was not so foolish she did not recognise a barb when it was directed towards her and she immediately looked mortified, but her demeanour changed just as rapidly at the arrival of the gentlemen some of whom appeared a little the worse for drink. Mademoiselle du Plessy lost no time in joining her husband-to-be and it was not long before, at her instigation, the servants began rolling up the beautiful Turkey carpets.

"Who shall play for us?" Lady Kirkland asked, glancing around the room.

"Why, Miss Winterton, of course," Veronique supplied with a smile. "I am told she is most accomplished.''

Davinia did not need to be asked twice. She immediately went to the spinet and began to sort through the music for suitable pieces. Several of the guests gravitated towards the card tables, but there were sufficient to make up sets for a country dance.

Davinia had always enjoyed playing the spinet and had entertained the Kirklands on several evenings since her arrival at the Manor. Without a doubt she would rather play for the entire evening than endure the fate which horrified Veronique du Plessy so much, for it was evident no gentleman would ask her to stand up with him.

The marquis quite naturally partnered his bride-to-be in the first set during which her father looked on, smiling with satisfaction. Davinia could not find it in her to blame him. Veronique du Plessy had achieved what many matchmaking mamas and ambitious daughters had failed to accomplish in many a year.

Much to Davinia's surprise the marquis stood up for only the country dance and immediately it had finished he crossed the room, offering to turn the pages of her music for the next piece, displacing one of Lizzie's would-be suitors. The gesture both pleased and embarrassed her. It evidently infuriated Veronique, for she flirted outrageously with all her subsequent partners be they young or old, something the marquis could not help but see.

Some time later, when another dance ended, Mademoiselle du Plessy happened to be standing close to the spinet in the company of one of the young men invited for Lizzie's sake. He was gazing wonderingly at the French girl as if he could not believe his good fortune in having such a fetching woman attending his words. Wearing a gown of peach satin with a low cut bodice and high waist, Davinia could readily acknowledge that she was a most beautiful woman. That she was also self-centered and petulant would be of no account to any gentleman caught up in her aura. In a gown of green velvet which Davinia had previously thought to be all the crack, she now felt quite shabby by comparison.

As the last note of music died away Davinia heard her say in a carrying tone, "Ravelston has such a kind heart, Mr. Livesey. He admires a pretty countenance, but he also exhibits the utmost charity to those less fortunately endowed."

Davinia longed to speak out and put the matter to rights. Lord Ravelston's kindness was based on his gratitude for her help when he was so ill, and nothing else. But Davinia made no retort after all and affected not to hear the unkind remark.

As she sorted through the music seeking a new tune to play she saw the marquis approaching her once again, this time accompanied by a bashful young woman of about Lizzie Moncrieff's age.

"You have played magnificently, Miss Winterton," he told her, "but the general opinion is that you deserve a respite."

She glanced up quickly and then away again. His presence always caused her heart to go a little wild, making her somewhat breathless. "I am quite happy to remain as long as everyone else wishes to dance."

"Ah, but there are those who would wish to stand up with you and Miss Carmichael has been gracious enough to offer to take your place."

Davinia had no choice but to give up her seat at the instrument. Politely, Lord Ravelston remained at the girl's side during the first piece which might have had some bearing on the wrong notes she played at frequent intervals.

Lady Kirkland was at the time playing piquet with Lord Castlereagh and when she caught sight of Davinia she beckoned her closer.

"Pray fetch my vinaigrette, my dear. It is so hot in here I can scarce draw breath."

"Shall I ask the servants to open some of the windows?"

The countess chuckled. "There would be a chorus of howls if you did, and half my guests would be in bed with chills on the morrow. Just fetch my vinaigrette; that will suffice."

Davinia took her time to go about the errand, knowing her mistress was not in dire need of being revived. When she returned with the vinaigrette some time later a lively gavotte was in progress and she sat down near the door in order to watch the dancers. Lord Ravelston partnered Mademoiselle du Plessy once again and she contrived to flirt with him throughout the set whenever the situation allowed. When it had finished a cotillion was announced and as the various gentlemen claimed their partners Davinia recalled how different life was at Kirkland Manor to that at Beech Tree Cottage where her existence had been so mundane. Evenings at Hindlesham Park were also quite different and nowhere near as lively. On those occasions when Davinia and her father had been invited up to the house, she had found it very tedious, with stilted conversation dominated by Lady Hindlesham, of course, and at best a rubber of whist to while away the evening.

"Miss Winterton." She looked up in alarm to find the marquis standing before her.

She smiled foolishly. "Oh, Lord Ravelston, I thought you were turning the pages of Miss Carmichael's music."

"I cannot be selfish and do so all evening, excluding others more worthy of the honour."

Davinia glanced across the room to where Lord Grindle had taken the marquis's place by the spinet, and then she returned her attention to him when he asked, "Will you do me the honour of standing up for the cotillion?"

For a few moments she felt confused, glancing around. Others were taking their places on the dance floor, including Mademoiselle du Plessy who was being partnered by Lord Kirkland on this occasion.

"Unless you are already engaged," he added, looking amused which irritated her, for he must know full well she was not.

"Lord Ravelston, there must be many of Lady Kirkland's guests who do not have a partner for this dance."

"They have all enjoyed an abundance of my attention this evening, ma'am. It is now your turn."

She stiffened with an anger she could not show. "I assure you there is no necessity for you to extend your magnanimity to *me*."

He was far from being disconcerted by her coolness and

his manner still appeared to be unruffled. "It surprises me to discover that your feathers are so easily ruffled."

"You mistake me," she scoffed.

"If that is so, it will give me the greatest pleasure to stand up with you, ma'am, and if you do not," he added in a gleeful whisper, "it will cause more comment than you would wish."

Several people nearby were glancing at them curiously, and, vexedly acknowledging the validity of his statement, Davinia gathered up her dignity and went with him to join the cotillion which was about to begin. It could not be often that a paid companion took her place with her mistress's guests, and Mademoiselle du Plessy cast them both a vexed look before bestowing one of her dazzling smiles upon her partner.

Davinia knew by comparison she must appear far from delighted at the honour bestowed upon her, and she was at a loss to know why. Normally the rare opportunity to dance would have been greeted with delight.

The cotillion was a lively dance and they had few opportunities to converse, but at one point Davinia could not help but remark, "You have a generous nature, my lord."

He appeared surprised at her comment. "That is something rarely attributed to me, Miss Winterton. What on earth prompts you to say so?"

She smiled quite genuinely now, recalling Veronique du Plessy's cruel remark. "You always find time to bestow your attention on those less fortunate or fair."

He frowned. "In truth, I cannot recall ever doing so, for I am at heart a selfish fellow who only enjoys the company of those well-endowed by nature."

She smiled again and from then onwards conversation was precluded. When the dance ended she curtseyed to her partner and he bowed before escorting her to the edge of the dance floor. During the dance she had made up her mind to retire unobtrusively from the gathering afterwards, knowing the party would go on long into the early hours, but before she had any opportunity to do so the Comte du Plessy approached. The thought of dancing with him repulsed her, for his hands were pudgy and Davinia imagined they would always be damp. However, it soon transpired that this was not his wish either.

"Mademoiselle Winterton, I beg of you join me in a rubber of whist. You do play, I take it?"

"Oh, yes, but . . ."

"Lady Kirkland suggested you as a partner, and I would be honoured, truly honoured if you would agree to be my partner."

Davinia raised her eyes to him. Previously she had dismissed him as a man of no account, almost a buffoon, but when she looked into his eyes there was a calculating light in them and briefly she wondered if she had misjudged him. He suddenly appeared very shrewd indeed.

As she sat down at the card table, nodding affably to Mr Henley and Lady Castlereagh who were already seated there, she caught sight of Veronique leading her husband-to-be towards the terrace and then, no doubt, to the privacy of the shrubbery.

Not for the first time did Davinia admit to herself that they were a handsome pair, before she sighed almost indiscernibly and applied herself to the game which was about to begin.

EIGHT

"Lord Kirkland has caught the most enormous carp, Mama," Lizzie Moncrieff announced the following morning.

She was standing by a window in the summer house which afforded an excellent view of the lake and the gentlemen who were fishing there. As well as Lizzie Moncrieff and her mother, several other ladies were sitting there, too.

At her daughter's remark Lady Kirkland looked up wearily. "Lizzie, my dear, I do wish you would learn to call him Papa. He would like it so much if you could find it in your heart to do so."

Lizzie glowered and it was as well her mother was sitting with her back towards her. "But he is not my papa."

"He is a good deal more worthy and deserving of more affection than you will bestow."

The girl looked vexed. "I will try, Mama," she replied with no real conviction in her voice.

Lady Kirkland looked immediately relieved. "How pleasant this is," she murmured, glancing round at all those present.

"I'd as lief be fishing at the lake than be here," her daughter responded.

"It would not be seemly. Fishing is a gentleman's pursuit, not that of a lady," the countess told her.

"Who decrees what is seemly and what is not?" Lizzie asked imperiously. "I am sure I would like to know."

"What a foolish question," her mother replied, looking irritated at last.

The girl shrugged her shoulders and then hugged her arms about her. "Oh, how I wish I were a gentleman and able to do just as I wish."

"I never envy gentlemen their pursuits," Veronique du Plessy declared.

She was wearing a white muslin gown, the only splash of colour a pink sash, and the rosebuds around the crown of her chipstraw bonnet. Davinia, who was quietly sewing in one corner, thought she looked absolutely beautiful, almost doll-like.

"Men have so much more freedom and enjoyment," Lizzie countered. "Nothing is beyond their reach."

"That is of no concern to me," the other girl declared. "I wish only to undertake womanly duties. What do you say, Miss Winterton? Do you not agree with me that being a woman is the most delightful thing?"

Davinia looked up from her sewing. "I have not thought on the matter to any degree, ma'am, but I am content as a woman and always have been."

Veronique du Plessy drew a deep sigh of satisfaction. "It is enough to love and be loved in return. It is all anyone would wish. Do you not also agree with that, Miss Winterton?"

Davinia was immediately discomforted, for no gentleman loved her or was likely to; somehow she felt Veronique du Plessy knew that and meant to discompose her.

"For some it is undoubtedly all that matters," Davinia murmured and returned her attention to her sewing.

"You will understand one day, Miss Moncrieff," the French girl told her, evidently determined not to let the subject alone, "if you set out to be amiable, that is."

Lizzie looked plainly scornful, but on a warning glance from her mother remained silent.

"Are you looking forward to setting up your own establishment, mademoiselle?" Lady Castlereagh enquired.

"Very much, my lady." The girl's eyes grew wide. "I hope to hold brilliant diversions next Season, but I am so inexperienced in those matters. Mayhap Lady Kirkland will be kind enough to guide me, as I have no mama to do so."

The countess cast her an absent smile. "Oh, I am persuaded you will contrive handsomely, my dear."

"You are very kind and it is true I have been mistress of my father's house ever since I have been old enough to act as hostess, although nowadays our home is not such a splendid one. In France, Papa owned two *chateaux* as well as a splendid *hôtel* in Paris." She sighed. "Papa grieves so much the loss of his possessions. He can find no solace."

"But he has his life," Lady Castlereagh pointed out, "which is of far more value."

"There are times when I believe Papa would rather have died than lose everything. We ate from gold plates and had a thousand servants before the revolution."

"And now you can have no more than a dozen," Lizzie pointed out gleefully. "How dreadful it must be for you."

"It is a truly dreadful situation," Lady Kirkland agreed. "And there are so many *emigrés* in a similar position. London is full of them at present." She smiled at Lady Castlereagh then. "I am gratified to see Lord Castlereagh looking a little better for his sojourn in the country, ma'am. I am persuaded you will agree with me."

The viscountess smiled although she looked rather strained. "It has, I believe, improved his health, but there are so many worries which plague him. He bears such a burden."

"Are we no nearer to winning the war?" Mrs Henley asked.

"Naturally," was Lady Castlereagh's indignant reply, "but my husband bears such a responsibility in that direction. Not only that but . . ."

Her voice trailed away as the others looked towards her hopefully. Lady Castlereagh averted her eyes. "You must forgive me; I cannot say more."

There was a momentary silence before Lizzie exclaimed, "Oh, it is monstrous! Those Frenchies are abominable and I hate them. I have heard tell they eat frogs and snails, and even candle-grease!"

Lady Kirkland shot her daughter a warning look, but it was too late. Veronique du Plessy cried, "That is so unfair! We do not," and burst into a noisy torrent of tears. Jumping to her feet she ran out of the summer house while the others, in stunned silence, watched her run down the hill towards the lake. As she approached Lord Ravelston he put down his fishing rod and got to his feet, looking worried and perplexed. Moments later he brought out his handkerchief and gave it to her before they both walked away from the others.

"Really, Lizzie, that was unforgivable!" her mother remonstrated. "Mademoiselle du Plessy is a guest in this house and you had no right to speak as you did in her presence. Indeed, you should not have made such cruel remarks at all!"

"Tush, Mama. She never minds hurting the sensibilities of others. I have often heard it myself."

"That is not to the point. You will apologise to her the first possible opportunity."

"Mama, I did not mean to insult *her*. She is an *emigré*, not a Frenchie."

"Nevertheless, you will apologise. I insist upon it."

The girl drew a deep sigh. "Yes, Mama."

"Now, go back to the house and stay in your room until I am able to speak with you later."

Lizzie looked downcast as she picked up her discarded bonnet by its strings. As she went out of the summer house Davinia quickly put away her sewing and got to her feet. "I will go with her, my lady."

"I trust you will not attempt to justify her insolence."

"No, indeed, my lady."

She curtseyed and a few moments later caught up with Lizzie who was marching purposefully towards the formal gardens. Lord Ravelston and Mademoiselle du Plessy could be seen walking slowly round the lake together, their heads inclined towards one another as he gave his betrothed his total attention.

Davinia could not help recall her near encounter with him early that morning. As was her custom she rose early, hours before the rest of the house party were likely to be up. Usually, on such occasions, she breakfasted in the servants' hall and was just making her way quietly downstairs when a noise arrested her. It was the sound of a door opening very carefully. Going forward slowly a few moments later she caught sight of the marquis, in his brocaded dressing gown, making his careful way back to his own room.

He did not see her and she wondered fleetingly which lady had been honoured by his company that night. Davinia was not surprised to find him out of his room, but she did think he might have tried to behave with more circumspection whilst his bride-to-be was under the same roof.

Lizzie Moncrieff glanced resentfully at her as Davinia fell into step at her side. "Has Mama sent you to castigate me, too?"

"Your conscience should be sufficient punishment, Miss Moncrieff. There is no need in my castigating you, too."

"Then you are to be my jailer."

Davinia looked at her in astonishment. "How can you say such a thing? I am merely returning to the house because I wish to have time on my own to reflect."

The girl cast her a curious look. "Reflect upon what, Miss Winterton?"

"Private matters."

Lizzie grinned. "A secret lover?"

"Miss Moncrieff," Davinia said with a laugh, "next Season you are to come out, which means there is a likelihood you will be wed within the twelve-month. Do you not think it time you became a little more demure and certainly less outspoken?''

''Would it be better if I were to make a cake of myself like Mademoiselle du Plessy with all her ridiculous airs and graces?''

''You have taken her in great dislike, have you not?''

''If you possessed an ounce of sensibility so would you. She has addressed horrid remarks to you.''

''I simply don't heed them.''

''You are truly remarkable to say so. I believe Ravelston has taken leave of his senses.''

''You are the only person who would venture such an opinion.''

''I am one of the few who knows him well.''

''Mademoiselle du Plessy is quite beautiful and amiable, too.''

''I cannot grant that, Miss Winterton. Fair curls are so unfashionable now, and as for her amiability . . .''

''A countenance like that possessed by Mademoiselle du Plessy is never out of fashion, Miss Moncrieff, and I'm persuaded you would take any female he wished to marry in dislike.''

''That is not true. A Season ago he paid court to Madeleine Chantrey who is the dearest person, but Ravelston didn't come up to scratch and she is now leg-shackled to someone else.''

After a moment's consideration, Davinia said, ''I am fully aware of how fond you are of Lord Ravelston, but if you wish to retain his friendship, Miss Moncrieff, you will be obliged to learn to accept his choice of bride.''

''Can *you*, Miss Winterton?''

Davinia laughed uneasily as they arrived back at the house. ''It is not for me to have any feelings on the matter.''

Lizzie grinned at her. ''Not even if you're wearing the willow for him?''

Davinia stepped back a pace, her heart leaping with alarm. "Miss Moncrieff, you do not know what you are saying!"

The girl chuckled. "Your face has grown red. You cannot hide it from me you know. I see *everything*."

" 'Tis a warm day which accounts for the colour in my cheeks. I beg of you do not ever speak such nonsense again. You read far too many novels and I fear your imagination goes beyond what is possible in real life. A hidden passion, indeed. Miss Moncrieff, you are indeed foolish."

The girl chuckled again, not at all put out. "Such moonshine. Do you consider that I am not up to snuff?"

Davinia laughed brokenly. "I would not be so foolish, but you are entirely wrong on this occasion."

"Oh no, I am not. 'Tis more than evident to me, Miss Winterton, and your feelings do you credit. You know him only as a rake but I assure you there is more to Rupert Ravelston than is ever apparent to others. Have no fear, your secret is safe with me."

Lizzie skipped into the house, leaving Davinia feeling stunned and distressed. After a moment she untied the strings of her bonnet and sank back against the wall, staring unseeingly into the formal garden. If Lizzie Moncrieff had guessed her secret, life could become rather trying from now on, she thought. More worrying was the fact that if Lizzie could guess, others might, too.

Davinia lost count of how long she remained there, allowing her thoughts to run riot in her head, but when she heard the unmistakable voice of Veronique du Plessy she became animated once more.

"I was never more mortified," the girl complained. "How dare she speak to me in such a fashion? That child is a veritable *enfant terrible*."

"My dear Veronique," came the marquis's reply, "if Lizzie sees that you are overset by her nonsense, she will try all the harder to discompose you."

"I suppose you condone such behaviour." Her voice sounded shrill and petulant.

"Not at all, my love," he answered soothingly, "but you must not allow her to discompose you so easily. It is by way of a sport with her."

"I am well aware of *that*, but I am so easily injured."

"If it will satisfy you I shall have serious words with her."

"It is her wish to gain your attention at any cost, and I would not for anything grant her that."

"Then I am at a loss what to do, my love."

"You can do nothing; that is what vexes me most. And while we are able to talk privately—which is rare enough these days—I would like you to know she will not be welcome in our house when we are wed. Moreover, I believe Miss Moncrieff is, together with Lady Kirkland's companion, in a mind to overset my nerves whenever possible."

"What has Miss Winterton to do with this?"

"She is the instigator of the irritation."

"I trust you are mistaken, my dear."

"I do not believe so. It is not the first time I have encountered the envy of women less fortunate than me."

"Well, you have so much to be envied, my love," was his reply.

"Am I always to expect such treatment?"

"In my experience you are usually treated with great reverence as is due to you. Lizzie is no more than a child."

"The same cannot be said for Miss Winterton."

"In all honesty, Veronique, I must entreat you to avoid her company if it teases you so much, and I want you to give your word you will not allow yourself to be discomposed by people who are of no consequence to our happiness."

Davinia did not wait to hear her reply, feeling guilty at eavesdropping and not liking what she had overheard. She slipped indoors before she could be seen.

Once again in the sanctuary of her small room on the second floor of the Manor, Davinia threw her bonnet on to the bed and went immediately to the dresser where she found the gold locket still wrapped in its concealing handkerchief. For a long moment she gazed at it cupped in her hands and then she opened it, looking down at the familiar golden curls. Unbidden tears came to her eyes and spilled on to her cheeks as she thought longingly of those days at Beech Troo Cottage where she shared a curious intimacy with a man called Rupert Jardine.

Lizzie had been correct, of course. Davinia acknowledged now she had foolishly lost her heart to a man who could never be true to any woman. Indeed, she should not allow herself to dwell upon the thought of it. When they removed to London for the coming Season it was going to be very difficult for her to see him leg-shackled to a vain and buffle-headed woman like Veronique du Plessy.

Lady Kirkland's discarded gowns were cut in such a fashion that they could contain no pocket but there was ample room over the bosom where Davinia secreted the locket within her shift so that at least a part of him would always be close to her heart.

NINE

The row of servants looked an impressive sight as they lined up in their bright liveries on the Broad Walk in front of the Manor. The peacocks which usually had it as their own domain had been banished for the time being. As well as the servants, all the Kirklands' guests were assembled there, too, clustered in small groups.

Lord Kirkland's under-butler was standing next to Evans, Lord Castlereagh's groom, and they were to race against Mr Monkswood's postillion and a dozen other servants, including Lord Ravelston's valet. Davinia understood such races were quite commonplace although this was the first she had ever witnessed. Wagers were being booked down and the matter was being taken very seriously indeed by all those present.

Mademoiselle du Plessy was wandering amongst the crowd gathered to witness the race and she appeared totally recovered from her earlier upset at the summer house. Davinia watched her as she twirled her parasol in a careless manner and smiled beguilingly at any gentleman who happened to catch her eye.

Lord Ravelston was in earnest conversation with Lord Castlereagh and from his gestures it appeared he was explaining the advantages possessed by his valet, although his expression was unusually serious. Every now and again Lord Castlereagh nodded with equal seriousness before shaking his head angrily and stalking away. The marquis scratched his head in apparent confusion before he shrugged his broad shoulders and walked in the opposite direction.

"You seem to have discomposed the Minister," Lord Kirkland challenged as the marquis approached.

Lord Ravelston grinned affably. "His lordship and I disagree over my claim to having the best man in the race. It is not so surprising. Everyone is crying roast meat over his own man. Not everyone can know as I do that Derringham can outstrip them all."

"Now who is crying roast meat?" Lord Kirkland declared laughingly.

"All those who are so disbelieving deserve to be relieved of their purses," the marquis retorted, good-naturedly.

"Stuff and nonsense!" cried Lord Grindle. "Only my man, Carnforth stands any chance at all."

"Believe what you will," the marquis told him. "We shall soon know who speaks with certain knowledge."

He glanced at Davinia and looked about to address some remark to her when Mr Monkswood slapped him on the back and declared, "I must naturally put my money on m'own man, but if I were to choose another, yours would be he, Ravelston. After all he is bound to be exceeding fit after helping you escape from the wrath of countless cuckolded husbands."

Everyone laughed except Davinia who was forcibly reminded of the dire results of one such escape.

Veronique came sauntering up to them, asking, "What is so amusing, gentlemen?"

"It is not for your dainty ears, m'dear," Lord Kirkland replied.

She looked slightly miffed and pouted. "If that is so I have a mind to withdraw my support of your man, Ravelston."

"Oh, I pray you do not," he begged, laughing anew, "although mayhap you should wager on Monsieur du Plessy's man."

"He is an ox. He will never win."

"Hush," the marquis urged. "Mrs Henley has ventured a guinea," a revelation which caused Veronique to laugh.

"What a chuckle-head she must be."

"Your father's coachman is well-fancied, m'dear," Lord Kirkland told her. "You mustn't disregard him."

"I shall not, my lord, but I do have a great regard for my pin money."

Lord Grindle laughed. "My word, Ravelston, you have a gem here."

Once again the marquis glanced at Davinia. "Yes, my lord, I know it."

Lady Grindle herself joined the group then and asked, "Mademoiselle du Plessy, have you set a date for your wedding as yet?"

The girl gave the woman her attention at last. "No, my lady, but a decision will be made very soon." She laughed deprecatingly, casting her eye over the others. "Ravelston is so impatient we cannot delay a decision for much longer, I fear."

"Indeed why should you, my dear?" murmured Lady Grindle.

Veronique glanced at Lizzie who was affecting not to have noticed her. "Papa tells me how often marriages were arranged in his youth. How dreadful that must have been. I cannot conceive of such a thing."

"It is often so today," Lady Grindle pointed out and the French girl shuddered delicately.

"I declare for those who have no chance of attracting a husband by their own charms it is better to have a marriage arranged than to remain a spinster, pitied by all. I am grateful it has not been so for me."

"There are worse fates than to remain a spinster," Lady Grindle pointed out.

"I cannot think of one," was Veronique's response.

"Going to the guillotine?" Lizzie suggested innocently.
"But perhaps not."

Davinia quickly drew her away from the group before any
further mischief could be caused.

"She needs a dose of stirrup-oil," the girl confided as she
walked away unwillingly.

"You promised your mama you would behave."

"And so I shall, but I am not obliged to listen to her crying roast meat just because she has made the match of the
Season."

"To some that would be reason enough," Davinia
pointed out.

"She really is a very vulgar type of person beneath all the
condescension and pride. I only wonder Ravelston has not
seen it in her."

The race was begun by Lady Kirkland who discharged
one of her husband's pistols into the air. Lizzie's attention
was immediately attracted as she called out encouragement
to her step-father's man. Davinia drew back a little. The
race did not interest her although she was able to observe the
marquis the better whilst it was proceeding.

He was quite obviously the wrong man to fall in love
with, but there was no doubt she experienced great pleasure
at the mere sight of him. He was taller than most of the other
men present, and always dressed in the height of fashion. He
was something of a dandy, but one who refused to exhibit
the excesses of fashion enjoyed by so many of them.

If his presence caused her pleasure, there was pain, too.
As Lady Kirkland's companion most of the guests ignored
her presence entirely, and if he did not it was merely out of
gratitude. Had she met him for the first time at Kirkland
Manor, the chances of her falling in love with him were
small, but she had known him as an ordinary man and not
the Marquis of Ravelston. For most of the time Davinia only
thought of him as the man who had stayed with them at
Beech Tree Cottage.

It had gradually occurred to her that she was not enjoying the house party at all. Normally such gatherings were enjoyable and were over all too quickly. On this occasion the time passed much too slowly and it was disheartening to realise that once it was over, as a close friend of the Kirkland family, Lord Ravelston was likely to remain at the Manor, together with the comte and his daughter. There would be no end to the torment which was becoming more painful by the day.

A great cry went up as the race ended at the far end of the Broad Walk. Lizzie Moncrieff came running up to her, hardly able to contain her excitement at the outcome. "Is it not famous, Miss Winterton? Ravelston's valet has won. It was exactly as I believed. Did you wager on him?"

Davinia shook her head. "No, I'm afraid I didn't. I felt obliged to support Lord Kirkland's under-butler."

Lizzie pulled a wry face. "So did I. If I had not Mama would have given me another set-down, but I knew all the while it would be Ravelston's man who would win."

Davinia glanced across to where the marquis was delightedly tossing a purse full of coins to his valet and receiving the congratulations of others. The serious look he had on his face earlier might never have been.

"How marvellous that was," Veronique du Plessy remarked, coming up behind them. "I am so proud of my dear Ravelston."

"It was his valet who won," Davinia pointed out and then felt bound to add, "It's a pity those men had to run in the full glare of the sun."

Veronique shrugged eloquently. "But they are servants. It is of no account. They must do their master's bidding."

Just then Davinia caught sight of the comte, striding along in the wake of the others. His face was red and his eyes blazing with anger. It looked as if he might burst at any moment.

"Papa?" Veronique said in astonishment when she caught sight of him. "What is amiss?"

"Need you ask? That lazy, good for nothing creature. How dare he shame me like this? I'll thrash him within an inch of his life."

As he stormed away his daughter followed. A moment afterwards the comte paused again, addressed himself to his daughter which caused her to remain where she was and then to turn away as he hurried on.

"Well, who would have thought he could be such a bad loser?" Lizzie exclaimed.

Davinia frowned. "He cannot be serious about thrashing his coachman."

"He looked exceeding serious to me."

Davinia looked at her. "Do you really think he will carry out that threat, truly, Miss Moncrieff?"

"I shouldn't doubt it for a moment," the girl answered with an uncaring shrug before she wandered away to talk with Samuel Livesey who had been trying to attract her attention for some time.

When Davinia glanced around everyone was intent upon discussing the race and no one else seemed to have been put out of countenance by their lost wagers. Veronique du Plessy was laughingly in conversation with a group of guests and seemed no longer concerned with her father's anger. Davinia bit her lip apprehensively and after a moment hurried away, taking the same direction as the comte.

The path led to the stable yard which was curiously deserted. No doubt the servants were counting their losses, too. After pausing there uncertainly for a moment or two Davinia heard a cry and a flow of French invective she couldn't begin to follow but she strode forward purposefully. There cowering in a corner of an empty stall was one of the losing runners and towering over him was the comte brandishing a horse-whip.

"No, no, monsieur," the man cried. "I could not help it. Derringham was too fast for me."

"I will teach you a lesson you will never forget!" the comte cried, beside himself with anger and quite deaf to his servant's pleas.

"Stop it!" Davinia cried. "Stop this immediately."

The comte swung on his heel. "What are you doing here?" he demanded.

"You must restrain yourself, monsieur."

"Who are you to tell me what to do? This is none of your concern. Be gone with you."

"I must make it my concern," she replied, trying to keep calm in the face of the man's unreasoning anger. "This man is not an animal. Please leave him be; he has been punished enough by your wrath."

"I am warning you; if you do not leave immediately you will be obliged to witness a most unpleasant scene."

"You may be quite certain I have no intention of leaving until you put down that whip."

The comte's rage seemed to drain away a little although his coachman still cowered in the corner, and he came towards Davinia, a horrible smile on his lips. "I do not obey servants, pretty though they may be. I intend to ensure that they always obey me."

Davinia's breath was coming heavily then. She disliked his mood as much as she had feared his anger. "That is not the correct way to ensure obedience, monsieur."

The comte swung round on his heel then, lashing out at the man with the whip. The poor man cried out and Davinia jumped. Before the comte could lash out again she had leaped forward to try and wrest the whip from his hand.

"Don't you dare!" she cried, as angry as he now. "Give that whip to me."

Suddenly, as she struggled with the enormously strong Frenchman she was pinioned from behind. Still struggling helplessly Davinia found herself being swung into the air and deposited several yards away from the fray.

Almost giddy from the speed at which it had happened she steadied herself on the stall where one of the horses was neighing loudly. When the stable stopped spinning Davinia saw that it was the marquis who had swept her out of harm's way. Now he was approaching the comte himself.

"Dammit, Ravelston, you do not also intend to interfere with me, do you?"

The marquis seemed unperturbed, which was quite a contrast to Davinia whose heart was beating so hard it seemed it might easily burst.

"You may do as you wish in your own house, monsieur, but I happen to be aware that Lady Kirkland would be very grieved to know of it happening here, and she is our hostess, after all."

"My honour is at stake," the comte cried in outraged tones.

The marquis took the whip from him and Davinia drew a sigh of relief. "Here in England we don't thrash our servants, only our wives."

To Davinia's amazement the Frenchman began to laugh. His coachman straightened up, brushing off his clothes and then, a moment later, ran past them all and out into the yard.

"You are correct in that, Ravelston. Thrash Veronique often and she will appreciate it, I assure you."

As the comte walked past Davinia so great was her distaste of the man she was hard-pressed not to shrink away from him. He paused to glance at her before he passed by. "You will never become a good servant if you behave in such a manner."

She straightened her bonnet and answered indignantly, "I am not a servant, monsieur, nor shall I ever be."

"You delude yourself, woman."

When he had gone she turned to the marquis who was frowning. "I am obliged to you for your intervention, my lord, and I am persuaded so is Monsieur du Plessy's servant.''

"It was not a matter for your concern, Miss Winterton.''

Davinia's eyes grew wide, her indignation growing once more. "I could not stand by and watch him thrash that man.''

"Even so it would have been better had you not interfered.'' There was no sign of mockery or amusement in his manner now. He was deadly serious.

"You cannot possibly condone such behaviour.''

"You have just seen that I do not, but you are employed as Lady Kirkland's companion. All I ask is that you conduct yourself as such.''

"You are as bad as Monsieur du Plessy. Mayhap I should learn to know my place.''

"It would make life more agreeable if you did.''

Stung by his attitude Davinia straightened her bonnet once again, tightened the strings and then bobbed a curtsey. "Yes, my lord. I will attempt to be more subservient in the future.''

A hint of a smile touched his lips as he replied, "I take leave to doubt that.''

Turning on her heel Davinia could not see his half smile as she hurried back towards the house, impatiently brushing away the tears which involuntarily sprung to her eyes at his scolding.

TEN

It was not until she was changing for dinner that Davinia discovered the locket was no longer in her shift. She cried out loud in alarm as the discovery was made and then swiftly removed all her clothing to make certain it had not slipped. Finally she shook every garment in desperation. It was no longer in her clothing or anywhere she searched in her small room.

The stable, she thought immediately. It must have been lost during the struggle in the stable.

She dressed in an amazingly quick time and, tossing a shawl about her shoulders, hurried out of the room. At that time of the day the guests were resting in their rooms prior to dressing for dinner, and most of the servants were occupied in preparing for the meal, so she encountered no one on her way.

When she came across one of Lord Kirkland's stableboys Davinia explained her loss, but he had not heard of any such locket being found. Her heart sank. If she had lost it for good her heart would surely break, and she dreaded having to enquire of others if it had been found. The locket was a splendid and valuable piece and they were bound to speculate on how she had come by it.

When she reached the stable she began a painstaking search of the floor. It yielded no clue and Davinia realised she might well have lost the locket at any time that afternoon.

Her heart was full of despair when she made her way back to the house, so much so she scarce noticed the man plodding wearily around the lake. Suddenly, though, she did catch sight of him and realised immediately it was the comte's coachman.

By the time she went inside several guests had come down and one was the marquis. He saw her enter the room and she kept deliberately away from him, instead going to join Lizzie Moncrieff who was leafing through some sheets of music in a desultory manner.

As Davinia crossed the room the comte glanced at her and their eyes met. She could hardly repress a shudder, for his eyes seemed filled with malice and she acknowledged she had made an enemy in this man.

"You look downcast," the girl immediately observed. "I trust you did not wager too much money on Papa's underbutler."

"I am not a gamester."

"Nor am I, I confess, but a great amount was won and lost today. Lord Fontanel is quite out of countenance this evening, but Ravelston, as you might imagine, is in high snuff."

Davinia sighed. "At least someone has profited out of today's events. I fear the servants involved have not."

Lizzie giggled. "Such a to-do with the comte's coachman. I suppose you will have heard that he did not whip his servant after all. He has obliged him to run one hundred times around the lake instead, and he has installed his valet to count! Is that not famous?"

The girl chuckled again, but Davinia gasped in exasperation. "How cruel he is, and for no good reason that I can see."

"You mustn't let it put you out of countenance, Miss Winterton; it is the French way to be cruel. Oh, Ravel, there you are. Are you still crying roast meat over your good fortune?"

Davinia stiffened now that she was aware he approached but she kept her head averted as he replied, his voice quite near, "It is not merely good fortune. I chose my man for his physical superiority."

At this Davinia finally raised her eyes to meet his. "Just like a racehorse, in fact."

He was not confounded by her evident disapproval. "Very much so, Miss Winterton."

"Do you like my gown, Ravel?" Lizzie asked, turning around so he could admire it the better.

"You would look delightful in anything you chose to wear."

The girl threw back her head and laughed delightedly. "Your tongue is as ever well hung."

"I have been charged to tell you your mama wishes to have words with you without further delay."

Lizzie cast him a coy glance. "Are you certain you are not trying to be rid of me?"

"If that was my wish I have had a hundred opportunities to do so permanently in the past."

"I cannot help but feel you regard me as a tiresome child."

"Only when you behave as such."

"Which is?"

"*Now*. Your mama is in a fidge to speak with you, Lizzie."

Laughing, she hurried away and when she had gone Davinia took up the music and affected to glance through it as he leaned indolently against the spinet and displayed no anxiety to leave her side. After a moment, when the silence between them became onerous, she asked, "Are you aware that Monsieur le Comte's coachman is obliged to run one hundred times around the lake?"

"I have heard mention of it. I imagine he would have preferred the beating." He flicked open his snuff box and took a pinch before returning it to his pocket.

Davinia looked at him in amazement. "Do you condone such barbarism?" she demanded to know.

"Do you not know the answer to that question?" His manner was unusually cool towards her.

"The comte, I must tell you, is a monster," Davinia could not help but retort in low tones, and then recalling that the marquis would soon be his son-in-law her cheeks grew rather pink.

The marquis straightened up then and gazed down into her eyes. "I would advise you to keep that opinion to yourself, Miss Winterton."

It was, she thought, a real warning which made her understand at last how deeply in love with Veronique du Plessy he must be. With rare bitterness she wondered what the French girl would do if she knew he had been half killed by a cuckolded husband, and even now indulged in a liaison with some lady in this very house. The secrecy involved indicated it was again a married lady whose husband would not take kindly to the situation.

"How long do you intend to stay at Kirkland?" she asked, glancing at him again.

He smiled and she saw the mocking look in his eyes. "Until the comte and his daughter decide to leave."

Recalling his swift departure from Beech Tree Cottage, she retorted, "Evidently you have no urgent business awaiting you in London on this occasion."

He grinned roguishly which only added to her chagrin. "Everything which interests me is here at the present time."

"Miss Winterton—Davinia, dear, I have a gentleman who wishes desperately to make your acquaintance."

At the sound of Lady Kirkland's voice Davinia looked away from him to see her employer approaching with a young man in tow.

"Mr Kingston wishes to meet you, my dear. He has lately taken up the position of curate at Tollerton. I am persuaded you and he will have a deal to talk about."

The countess left the rather unimposing young man in Davinia's company and went off to converse with the more important of her guests. Davinia was hard put not to laugh at such a blatant piece of matchmaking, but she politely responded to the young man's rather dull conversation, not daring to look around to see if the marquis was still close by. A short time afterwards she noted he was once again at Veronique's side as he conversed with her and her father, and Davinia's heart ached anew.

The new curate was also seated next to Davinia at dinner and Lady Kirkland cast her frequent encouraging smiles as the meal progressed. Davinia did contrive to hold a lucid conversation with Mr Kingston, but all the while she was aware of the marquis not far away from her. Tonight he had been seated further down the table near his host and hostess and next to Lady Castlereagh, and he seemed able to keep up a constant stream of badinage with her. Emily Castlereagh seemed entranced, something Davinia could understand all too well. Every now and again the viscountess would erupt into laughter at something he had said.

Despite her awareness of him, however, Davinia's mind constantly dwelled upon the lost locket. If it proved to be lost for ever it would be too cruel.

As soon as the ladies retired to the drawing room after dinner, she slipped away and out of the house once more. As she approached the Broad Walk she caught sight of the comte's coachman being helped back to the stables by two other servants. He looked to be half dead and her anger was aroused anew.

However, her first concern just then was to find the locket. The problem was, it might have been lost anywhere within the very extensive grounds of Kirkland Manor, but she had been so certain the loss occurred in the stables during the struggle. Nevertheless, Davinia began her painstaking search, thankful for the long summer evenings which afforded sufficient light. Inch by inch she surveyed the ground to no avail, and when she was almost finished despair encroached upon her once more. She couldn't think where to look next.

Just when she was almost back to where she had begun she heard a scrunch on the gravel nearby and then a pair of brightly polished shoes came into view as she began to straighten up. Her eyes came level with a pair of immaculate buckskin breeches, then a dark blue evening coat. Before her eyes came level with his white linen shirt and perfectly folded neckcloth she saw the object negligently dangling from his fingers, glinting as it caught the last rays of the dying sun.

"Are you searching for this by any chance, Miss Winterton?"

Her heart was filled with fury that it should have been Lord Ravelston who found it. She would not have wished him to know she had coveted it so well.

"Where . . . where did you find it?" she managed to ask after a full minute's stunned silence.

"You dropped it in the stable this afternoon."

All at once her anger no longer could be contained. "Has it been in your possession all this time?"

"It has."

"Why did you not let me have it earlier?"

One of his eyebrows rose a little. "In front of everyone, Miss Winterton? Or perchance you would have preferred me to bring it to your room?"

Davinia reached out to snatch it from him, but he kept it just out of her reach. "I confess it was a great surprise to me to find it there, ma'am, for I quite clearly recall your declaration that it was totally improper for you to wear it."

Her cheeks grew pink. "Indeed I do not do any such thing. I merely . . . keep it by me for safety's sake."

"Evidently your precaution proved to be inadequate."

By this time she was feeling totally humiliated, but her chin came up proudly and she forced herself to look him in the eye, a difficult task in view of his mockery. "You are holding it as the devil would hug a witch, my lord."

"Naturally. I am fully aware of its value."

Davinia's breast was heaving with indignation. "In that event I suggest you keep it. It will be safer in your keeping. Indeed you should never have bestowed an object of such value upon so unworthy a recipient."

As she made to go past him he caught her arm and drew her back towards him. "I did not give it to you merely to have it returned, Miss Winterton," he said in a quiet voice. "Whatever your opinion of me I am truly grateful to you and wish you to have this small token of my regard."

"And if I do not accept it back?"

He cast her a smile which she thought might melt the hardest of hearts, let alone one which adored him. "I should be totally devastated."

Her own anger melted easily in the face of his practised charm. "I should not wish for that, my lord."

"Mayhap you would keep it safer in the future by wearing it," he suggested as she reached out to take it once more. "The clasp is quite a strong one so I doubt it would come loose."

Before she could demur he was fastening it around her neck. Her breath caught in her throat at his closeness and she recalled the time when she nursed him back to health and was near to him for hours on end. Now she began to tremble as he fastened the locket about her throat. His breath was cool on her neck.

"Is that not better, Miss Winterton?" he asked when it was done, his voice still close to her ear.

Davinia stepped back quickly so much so the heel of her slipper twisted beneath her and she almost stumbled. Before she could fall he had caught her arm and steadied her.

"I thank you," she said in an uneven voice.

"My pleasure, ma'am," he replied, eyeing her curiously.

"Having the locket back in my possession is a great relief," she admitted before glancing at him shyly.

"It is an honour to be of service to you, ma'am."

"I must return indoors; Lady Kirkland may be in need of me."

As she attempted to hurry away from this man who so easily discomposed her, he fell into step beside her, saying in a conversational tone, "Lady Kirkland is the last person I would have considered in need of a companion, delightful as she must find your company."

"I have not met any others who have companions, so I cannot say."

"I can, and it is most unlike her."

"Her sister died earlier this year and I am given to believe Lady Kirkland misses her companionship greatly."

"Ah yes, I recall the tragedy and you are undoubtedly correct."

"I consider myself the most fortunate creature alive to have such a situation."

The marquis was eyeing her with rare sobriety. "You have no need to praise Lady Kirkland to me. I have long been aware of her worth." Davinia recalled his nocturnal visit and hoped desperately the countess was not the recipient. "But do you look no further than a life as a paid companion, Miss Winterton?"

"I have no choice, my lord. I am quite satisfied, you may be sure."

They had re-entered the house and Davinia was more than a little grateful that they had managed to walk into the drawing room without attracting undue attention. The gentlemen had joined the ladies and one persistent matron was attempting to draw Viscount Castlereagh on matters pertaining to the war.

"When will this wretched business end, Lord Castlereagh?" she was demanding in a shrill voice.

"Does the war inconvenience you, ma'am?" the viscount enquired politely.

"My husband cannot obtain his favourite claret any longer and he becomes most vexed."

"I cannot say when the situation will improve," the minister replied, sounding bored. "It will be ended as soon as can be contrived, I assure you."

"I pray you are correct," the comte interpolated, "for I would one day wish to return to my country."

"When you do you will find life vastly changed, I fear," Mr Monkswood informed him, affecting a fashionably languid air.

The comte's answer was to glare at him. Lady Kirkland came hurrying up to Davinia, saying, "My dear, everyone is in a fidge to dance tonight, so pray oblige us by playing."

"It would be an honour," Davinia replied truthfully, glad of being occupied.

Lady Kirkland's glance immediately dropped to the locket which rested prominently on Davinia's breast. "What a pretty thing that is. I don't believe I have seen it before."

"I haven't worn it before, my lady."

"An heirloom, I don't doubt."

"Yes, it is," she replied, glancing across the room to where the marquis was in conversation with his bride-to-be and Mrs Henley.

"Such gee-gaws must not be hidden away. You must contrive to wear it more often."

Davinia smiled as she returned her attention to the countess. "Yes, I will, my lady."

As Lady Kirkland turned away she added as an afterthought, "Tomorrow morning I would have you drive into Tollerton for me. There are a number of items I need from the haberdasher although I am persuaded his stock is poor indeed compared to Fife's in Bond Street."

Davinia looked forward to the outing with great pleasure

and said so. "Take Lizzie with you," the countess added. "She will be better for being kept away from a certain person."

Davinia laughed. From where she was standing she could see that Lizzie had joined the marquis and the others, and was flirting with him outrageously, no doubt to the chagrin of Veronique du Plessy.

"Miss Moncrieff is always in such high snuff, my lady."

"There are times when I would wish her to be less of the hoyden, as I have often said, but where Ravelston is concerned I have no influence whatsoever. She has always treated him as a brother, and I fear this irrational dislike of Mademoiselle du Plessy bodes no good for any of us. Where Ravelston's choice of a bride is concerned Lizzie would find fault with a fat goose."

"You must not concern yourself on that score, my lady. Miss Moncrieff is not like to change Lord Ravelston's mind in that direction whatever she says or does."

Lady Kirkland looked indignant. "Indeed not. Ravelston is a most singularly minded person. Once set upon a course, nought is like to change it, although I confess after years of acquaintanceship with him he is still an enigma to me. Beneath his crack-brained antics, I am bound to speculate that there is quite another person, a man of kindness and sensitivity. One can only hope his bride will bring it out in him although I confess to you I have my doubts."

As she moved away Davinia was left thoughtful, for Lady Kirkland was the second person to intimate Lord Ravelston was not merely the scapegrace he appeared to be. After a moment, though, she went to the spinet and began to play whilst many of the guests sought out partners for the dancing. On this occasion Lord Ravelston did not intervene and once again it was not until late that the party broke up.

Davinia remained downstairs for some considerable time after most of the others had retired to their rooms. It had been an eventful day and she was far from feeling sleepy. A turn in the garden, inhaling the cool night air, was what she needed and she wandered aimlessly for a while aided by the moonlight which shone out of a cloudless sky. At last she did feel weary and made her slow way upstairs. The candles in the sconces which lined the corridors were burning low, giving off an eerie flickering light. There were colourful stories of long-dead Kirklands who still walked the corridors of the Manor, told to Davinia on her arrival by a gleeful Lizzie.

As far as Davinia knew, only fanciful maidservants had ever admitted to seeing a spectre, but all the same when the house was quiet and the old timbers creaked, she realised it was easy to be fanciful and she wished she had retired at the same time as everyone else.

Suddenly she froze in terror as a floorboard creaked nearby. Davinia shrank into a recess, drawing her shawl around her in fear. A moment later a shadow loomed in front of her followed by the reality—the marquis. Davinia almost cried out in exasperation but contrived to remain unseen as he furtively went on his way. Fascinated and guilty at the same time she continued to watch his progress until he hesitated outside one particular door.

Davinia had assisted Lady Kirkland in assigning the rooms to her guests but she could not recall them all. He paused to glance around him, then after a moment or two the bedroom door opened and the marquis went inside. For a few minutes Davinia remained in the recess, stunned by what she had seen, for the person who had admitted the marquis to her bedchamber was none other than Emily Castlereagh, a partner in a marriage which was considered perfect. That the War Minister's wife should be his secret mistress was one of the most disturbing facts she had ever learned about him. To Davinia's mind it was akin to treason.

ELEVEN

The ride to Tollerton the following morning was a pleasant one. The town was situated some six miles from Kirkland and its attached village, through pretty countryside. Lady Kirkland's carriage was well-sprung but Davinia did after all make the journey alone.

Lizzie Moncrieff, no doubt suspecting her mother's guile, affected a headache although she was, in fact, busily trying to fade her countless freckles with lemon juice and cucumber when Davinia approached her.

"What a curse these blemishes are," she moaned as Davinia entered her room.

"They can look fetching," Davinia told her.

Lizzie laughed. "Not on an already plain countenance. Oh, Miss Winterton, my head truly aches abominably and I really cannot face a carriage ride, however pleasant it might be."

Davinia cast her a disbelieving look. "If you are so badly afflicted, I fear you will be obliged to remain in your room for the rest of the day."

"I shall take a dose of laudanum which relieves the headache very quickly. In any event Lord Kirkland has heard bad weather is coming and he has brought forward the shoot to today. It will be most uninteresting, so I shall be missing nothing of any import."

In all truth, Davinia was not sorry to be alone. Lizzie was far too sharp for comfort and Davinia could readily understand Lady Kirkland's anxiety and her desire to find her daughter a husband as soon as possible.

A pleasant hour went by as Davinia purchased all the ribbons and sewing silks Lady Kirkland required. She also purchased an item or two herself—some handkerchiefs to embroider during the less hectic days to come.

Just as she came out of the haberdasher's shop Mr Kingston, the curate, was walking across the road towards her and Davinia greeted him with true warmth.

"Mr Kingston, how nice it is to see you again and so soon."

He seemed equally pleased to see her. "This is truly good fortune, Miss Winterton. I trust you are well today."

"Indeed, I am in rude health and engaged upon an errand for Lady Kirkland."

"Ah, she is a lady of rare sensibility. I hold her in the highest regard."

"Mayhap we shall see you again at the Manor before very long, Mr Kingston."

"Whenever Lord and Lady Kirkland condescend to invite me, but mayhap we shall see you in church this coming Sunday."

"Indeed you will, sir."

He tipped his hat. "Until then, Miss Winterton."

Still smiling she watched him walk down the street and then froze a few moments later when she caught sight of a familiar figure coming out of the inn. The swaggering walk was unmistakable as he paused and then moved forward to glance up and down the street. Inevitably he did catch sight of her and deep in her heart she was not sorry. Every moment spent with him, even though they invariably disagreed, was one to be treasured.

His face remained expressionless as he gazed across at her and then, after a farmer's cart had passed by, he came towards her sporting the familiar devil-may-care attitude she had grown accustomed to.

"Good day to you, Miss Winterton! What happy chance brings you to Tollerton?"

"I am on an errand for Lady Kirkland. She was in no mind to leave her guests."

Several well-dressed gentlemen came out of the inn, glanced across at the marquis who had his back towards them, and hurried away towards the livery stable. The marquis seemed totally unaware of them as he gazed at Davinia. Once the men had gone she returned her attention to him.

"Are you with any other of Lord and Lady Kirkland's guests? I would not wish to keep you from them."

He smiled. "You have caught me out, Miss Winterton. Dare I beg your discretion on yet another occasion?" Unwillingly she stiffened as he went on in a confidential tone, "Being the unprincipled creature that I am, I felt the need to consort with my less elevated cronies." He lowered his voice even more. "Somehow the landlord of this excellent establishment is in possession of some superior brandy, and I was fortunate enough to come to know of it."

She cast him a vexed look. "Is it not early in the day to be imbibing, my lord?"

The marquis laughed. "It is never too early to enjoy the company of a comely female or a fine wine."

"You seem intent upon enjoying both, my lord."

"Indeed, I can think of no finer pursuits in life. I note that the local curate is of a similar mind. At least he appears to prefer a comely female to a good wine, and who is to say his bias is the wrong one?"

Davinia's cheeks grew pink. She was beginning to despise her habit of blushing so readily. Noting it the marquis added, "I see the good country air has benefited your health."

"There is nothing wrong with my health, Lord Ravelston."

"That is an unfashionable attitude."

"I am an unfashionable woman."

"Oh, most delightfully so. The habit of languor does not find favour with me."

She began to turn away. Far from enjoying the conversation she disliked the obvious meaninglessness of it and his habitual teasing was beginning to grate.

"I am persuaded it has not escaped your notice that we seem to be fated to meet often," he added in a more serious tone.

"In view of your pursuits, you must regard it as a great misfortune."

"Only on some occasions; by no means all. However you will soon be freed of such a vexation, for I shall be leaving Kirkland Manor before long." On hearing this piece of unexpected information Davinia looked alarmed. "Several of us have made up our minds to return to London within the next few days."

Davinia was suddenly desolate but she still dare not let her feelings show. "Your reason for such a hasty departure is evident, my lord."

He looked surprised. "I was not aware of that, Miss Winterton. You must be exceeding observant."

Feeling uncomfortable she went on to explain. "It is evident you are anxious to prepare for your bride. There is much to be done prior to any nuptials and everyone is anxiously awaiting the wedding itself."

His eyes bore a curious expression. "Are they indeed? Seeing a man become leg-shackled is almost as entertaining as watching a public execution at Newgate."

She affected a bright smile, not knowing whether she was expected to laugh at his witticism or not. "Mademoiselle du Plessy is promising remarkable diversions next Season."

"They might not be quite as everyone imagines."

At such an enigmatic statement she cast him a curious glance, for he appeared to be in an odd humour now. After a moment, to make more easy conversation, she said, "It has been a most diverting time of late."

"What a pity it will all soon be ended," he answered, his lips twisting into the semblance of a smile.

She looked surprised. "All? I did not know of that. Is everyone else to leave, too?"

"You evidently have not heard that Lord Castlereagh has been recalled to London and leaves on the morrow. I have no doubt when he leaves others will follow, and as I have said, I, too, have made up my mind to leave."

Davinia wondered if matters of state beckoned the Minister, or something of a more personal nature drove him away from Kirkland Manor. In any event it seemed clear that Lord Ravelston intended to follow. He really was beyond remedy and Mademoiselle du Plessy was not to be envied at all.

"I had not heard," she replied, "but that may in part explain why Lord Kirkland has brought forward the duck shoot to this afternoon. Miss Moncrieff thought it might be the weather, but evidently it was this other consideration which must have weighed with him."

His entire demeanour changed on hearing this piece of information. "Are you quite certain of this?"

"Miss Moncrieff told me so only this morning, and I have no reason to doubt her word."

The marquis appeared stunned and was thoughtful for a moment before he said, "I must return to Kirkland Manor immediately."

"You are not like to miss it, my lord, for there is to be a picnic before it begins."

He reached out to touch her arm, his mind obviously still preoccupied with what she had told him. "Miss Winterton, I am most obliged to you for this information."

So saying he ran back across the road, leaving her looking totally bemused. Just as she made to return to the waiting carriage he came riding out of the inn courtyard at a hard gallop, waving to her briefly as he passed by.

Standing by the carriage, Davinia watched him go, his fair curls ruffled by the wind, his cloak billowing out behind him. Then she sighed and climbed into the carriage. As the footman helped her inside, she asked, "Do you know how Monsieur du Plessy's coachman is this morning?"

"Recovering, ma'am. We gave him some gin and today he's bosky. He'll ride grub for the next few days, but he's not had notice to quit because of his exertion."

"Not on this occasion," Davinia answered grimly, "but the comte was as mad as a weaver and like to kill someone one day when he's in a similar mood."

"Well, it's not for me to say, ma'am, but seeing you're in the way of being one of us it mightn't matter. All Monsieur du Plessy's servants live in fear of him. They are regularly beaten if they displease."

The information did not surprise her, but as an afterthought she asked, "Does that include Mademoiselle du Plessy's maid?"

"Yes, ma'am. Mademoiselle du Plessy beats poor Fanny regularly. The girl's for ever weeping because of it."

As she rode back to Kirkland Manor Davinia was angry again at the thought of the comte's servants being punished so severely, but one consolation was the knowledge that after their marriage Lord Ravelston would prevent it happening to his wife's maid. At least, Davinia was almost certain he would.

The picnic was being loaded on to wagons by the servants when she arrived back at Kirkland Manor. Lady Kirkland declared herself delighted with Davinia's purchases, amazed that they could be obtained at all in Tollerton, and then she rushed away to prepare for the afternoon's diversion. Davinia had no intention of joining the shoot and was on her way to her room when she encountered the marquis once again.

"Are you not ready for the picnic, Miss Winterton?"

"I am not a good shot, Lord Ravelston. I see no advantage in my joining the picnic if I am not to go along with the shoot."

"Few of the ladies will be shooting, but you may carry my powder if you wish."

Davinia grinned crookedly. "Oh, I am persuaded you will have any number of females, not only wishing to carry your powder, but your fowling piece, too."

Lord and Lady Castlereagh came out of their rooms at that point, nodding pleasantly towards Davinia and the marquis. His expression as he stared after the couple was a strange one, almost brooding.

As Davinia turned to leave him he asked, "Do you never wonder if you misjudge me?"

Startled she replied, "Lord Ravelston, a creature such as I would never presume to judge you at all."

He caught her arm and she was startled again to find him angry. "Don't be missish with me, madam."

With slow deliberation she drew away from him. "I beg of you forget our previous acquaintanceship, and I implore you to treat me as another of Lady Kirkland's servants."

"Would your damnable pride tolerate such treatment?"

"I cannot afford that luxury as you well know and I have it in mind that you regard me as some kind of sport."

"You cannot be more wrong."

"If that is so I would beg your pardon most humbly."

"Now you are teasing me."

"I would not presume to do so. In any event, I couldn't hope to emulate your skill at mockery which is so well practised."

"I wish you would not despise me so."

"I am honoured you care a fig what I think of you, my lord, but I assure you your behaviour or its result is of no consequence to me."

His face grew dark with anger again and Davinia wondered why she had spoken with such severity. The answer came to her swiftly; she was intent upon hiding her true feeling for him at all times.

"Then mayhap you will find this of some consequence."

He caught hold of her again before she had a chance to evade him. Pulling her towards him he held her tight in his arms so that she could not escape. The pungent odour of his eau de cologne made her head swim.

"Oh, please . . ." she begged, struggling feebly to free herself, but he pressed his lips to hers despite her plea.

The sensation was so delightful she immediately ceased to struggle, lost only in the pleasure of his embrace. At last, however, she drew away, horrified at the wantonness of her own behaviour.

"Davinia," he began, using her name for the first time. There was no mockery in his demeanour, but she was in no mood to realise that.

"How dare you?" she gasped, and to her chagrin he laughed.

Furiously she lashed out at him, but he deflected her hand easily. "I am not to be trifled with like a housemaid."

He was still laughing as he replied, "I was not trifling with you."

"Have you forgotten your bride-to-be?"

His laughter faded and his eyes seemed to grow very dark. "I have forgotten nothing."

"Ravelston! *Chéri*," called a familiar voice. "Papa is waiting for you in the gun room. Have you forgotten?"

"How could I?" he responded with a joviality Davinia could not credit.

The man must be a greater actor than Edmund Kean himself, she thought, as she turned away from him, her heart beating fast. Mademoiselle du Plessy came hurrying along the corridor, fastening her pelisse. The girl's expectant smile faded a little when she caught sight of Davinia.

"Miss Winterton," she said stiffly.

Davinia nodded to her and quickly excused herself, aware that both the marquis and Veronique du Plessy were watching her as she hurried down the stairs and as far away from them as she could get.

TWELVE

In an attempt to avoid contact with anyone else until she had regained her composure Davinia hurried out into the garden where the air felt cool upon her hot cheeks. It seemed very important that no one should clap eyes upon her, for she felt his kisses must be marked indelibly upon her face and anyone looking at her would surely see them. Still racked from the passion of his embrace and her own response to it, Davinia wiped away a surreptitious tear, refusing to have her heart broken by a man who regarded every female he happened upon as a challenge to be overcome. He was nothing but a heartless rake.

The worst aspect of the matter was that she still loved him in spite of it, knowing he was unlikely to be true even to Mademoiselle du Plessy, which was no consolation.

Davinia sank down on to a rustic seat, her heart heavy. Next Season when she would accompany the Kirklands to London was bound to be painful, encountering the newly-wed marquis at every turn. It was going to be especially disagreeable now that she had allowed her own wantonness to be so apparent to him. His mockery and teasing was likely to gain momentum each time they met. She recalled the mildly romantic notion she had harboured for Sir George Hindlesham. How foolish that seemed in retrospect. How mild by comparison to this raging fever she had in her heart. It distressed her to recall she might well have married Sir George had he offered for her.

The sound of footsteps slowly approaching caused her to freeze, fearful in the event Lord Ravelston had come to seek her out for more of his heartless teasing. However, it was fortunate she was well-concealed in an arbour and Davinia knew if she stayed very quiet it was likely he would go away and she could remain undiscovered until the shooting party had left for the picnic.

"I think it has turned out to be a deal of nonsense after all, Monkswood, and if you had an ounce of sense you would realise it, too."

At the sound of the War Minister's voice, Davinia realised she had committed an error.

"The warning came from a reliable source," Mr Monkswood replied. "You would do well to heed it."

"I am well acquainted with your source, remember, but even he is like to be mistaken now and again."

"My lord," the other man said, with infinite patience, "we have all known for some months past that there is like to be an attempt upon your life . . ."

Davinia shrank further down on the seat, pressing one hand to her lips to prevent a cry escaping them. She knew full well this was one conversation she had no right to overhear, but if she were to go now she was bound to reveal her presence to them.

"If that is so, why has it not been done by now?" the Minister demanded.

"Opportunity, my lord, or more like the lack of it."

"Faddle, Monkswood. There has been ample opportunity both here and in London."

"He would not wish to put his own life in danger, and you have been well protected since the matter became known to us."

"I really do not feel justified in curtailing my pleasure." The Minister for War sounded thoughtful.

"You must on this occasion, my lord. We are talking

about a man who is both dangerous and dedicated, not a crazed lunatic escaped from Bedlam.''

''Over the past few days, since he was introduced to me, I have conversed with him on several occasions and I am bound to say he appears to be quite an amiable fellow.''

Mr Monkswood laughed deprecatingly. ''My lord, he might act the buffoon, but I assure you quite the opposite is true. He is a crack shot and totally ruthless. What could be better for his purpose than a shooting accident? In such circumstances it couldn't be determined who had fired the actual shot. It is the perfect opportunity and one I don't doubt he has been waiting for. I am persuaded the danger is very real. We have been observing him closely of late. He had a rendezvous with French agents only recently in the nearby town . . .''

As they began to walk away, back towards the house, Davinia remained where she was, trapped by fear and apprehension. It seemed evident to whom they referred and it made her blood run cold, but at least she knew now why Lord Ravelston's behaviour had often puzzled her. It was an act after all, and one calculated to mask a greater evil.

All at once she jumped to her feet and ran back towards the house, aware only that she had to stop it. Whatever the marquis's motive in wanting to assassinate the viscount, he must not be allowed to succeed.

The last carriage was just about to leave as Davinia raced on to the drive holding up her skirts and dangling her bonnet by its strings. Breathlessly she sank back into the squabs to discover she was sharing a carriage with Mademoiselle du Plessy, her father and Mr and Mrs Henley.

''My dear Miss Winterton, it is quite unlike you to be tardy,'' Mrs Henley declared as Davinia endeavoured to catch her breath.

''A small matter detained me,'' she gasped.

''No doubt the lackey who looks upon you so favourably,'' Veronique du Plessy commented, smiling coldly. ''You really should be more considerate. A match would be suitable for one of your station."

"I cannot conceive what you may mean," Davinia responded stiffly.

"Such modesty."

"I was always taught modesty is one of the most redeeming features in a lady."

Veronique du Plessy looked vexed but after all she had overheard, Davinia couldn't care less about a few overset sensibilities.

"How true that is," cooed Mrs Henley, apparently unaware of any tension between the two younger women. "So many young ladies today are too forward by far. This fashion for dampening shifts is quite *outré*."

As it was evident Veronique du Plessy adopted this fashion to draw attention to her ample curves Davinia was amused, although she did not show it. The French girl, however, continued to look miffed.

"Is not Lord Ravelston with you?" Davinia asked, deciding on this occasion curiosity was much better than reticence. "It is so rare to find him far from your side."

"He is riding ahead on horseback with Lord Kirkland and Lord Fontanel. I cannot expect him to stick like wax at all times, even though we are betrothed. No sophisticated lady would think to do so."

From her tone it seemed evident that was precisely what she did wish, but Mrs Henley was quick to agree. "That is very sensible of you, dear. Lord Ravelston is one gentleman who would not wish to be kept on leading strings."

Her husband chuckled. "That is precisely what you have done to me, my dear."

"Ah, but you are not Lord Ravelston," was her sage reply.

Monsieur du Plessy was sitting in the corner of the carriage, not troubling to join in the conversation. Glancing at him curiously, Davinia decided he looked to be in a bad humour and fleetingly wondered why. All in all he seemed a most disagreeable man.

The carriage didn't take long to arrive at the glade by the riverside which had been chosen for its sylvan setting as the picnic site. Most of the guests had already arrived and the liveried footmen were unpacking the food and setting it out for everyone's enjoyment. Lady Kirkland looked lovely in her muslin gown and flower-bedecked bonnet as she moved amongst her guests. At that moment Davinia envied her lightheartedness.

"I thought you had made up your mind not to join us," she remarked when she caught sight of Davinia.

"It is such a fine day I deemed it a pity to miss the picnic."

The countess glanced doubtfully at the sky. "One can only hope the weather remains fine."

At the same time Davinia wished for a deluge, even though she knew it would only delay the inevitable calamity.

During the picnic she was horrified to note that not only was the marquis in high spirits, he was also a member of Lord Castlereagh's select little group. As before, he flirted outrageously with Emily Castlereagh, and Davinia could only wonder why her husband appeared heedless of it. No doubt the threat to his life occupied most of his thoughts, as well as the conduct of the war which must weigh heavily upon him. Davinia could think of nothing else except the conversation she had overheard even to the extent of trying to put another construction upon it, but alas their words were plain enough.

"The Prince of Wales has behaved outrageously towards poor Princess Caroline, I feel," Lady Grindle was saying as she delicately chewed on a chicken leg.

"The princess herself has behaved no better," another lady answered. "I have the confidence of one of her ladies in waiting and Lord Canning is involved with her now. It is even rumoured that this child she has with her, is her own and cannot possibly be the Prince's. As a result there is to be a delicate investigation of the whole affair, but Lord Castlereagh will not reveal his thoughts on the matter. I have endeavoured to persuade him, to no avail.''

The interminable picnic was over at last. Davinia had not been able to eat a morsel of the delicious collation, a fact commented upon by Ariadne Henley.

''Miss Winterton, you have scarce eaten. The weather is not as fine as it might be and I trust you are not sickening for a chill.''

Davinia managed a reassuring smile. ''I think not, ma'am. The air is a trifle close, but I don't believe it has affected me overmuch, although I thank you for your concern.''

Mrs Henley looked up at the clouds which were thickening and beginning to darken the sky. ''I fear we shall have a storm before the day is over.''

''As long as the men get in their shooting first,'' Lady Grindle remarked. ''The storm would surely not dare to break before then!''

Those within earshot laughed. Davinia kept casting nervous looks towards the marquis who seemed as usual remarkably lighthearted. Once or twice he had cast her a curious look. He was never very far from the Castlereaghs it seemed, something she had only just begun to notice.

When the shooting party began to assemble and the dogs arrived with their handlers Davinia wandered off to join them. Nearby, the servants struggled to restrain the dogs which were anxious to be away to their sport. Most of the ladies were to remain at the glade, to gossip or to sew. Lizzie, who was quite recovered from her headache, was about to play hide and seek with her friends and was in high spirits. Davinia wondered what her reaction would be if she knew her adored Ravelston was such an evil creature.

The marquis looked far from pleased at seeing Davinia,

but she remained heedless of his disapproval. "I believed you intended not to come," he said, affecting a cold manner.

"How ungracious of you, Lord Ravelston. I thought you wanted someone to carry your shot."

"One of the servants can do so quite easily."

She smiled at him coyly. "Evidently you didn't intend your offer to be taken up."

His expression softened somewhat then. "When you refused I was of course devastated, but I recovered sufficiently to make alternative arrangements which cannot now be undone."

She gazed at him admiringly. "You lie as fast as a dog can trot," she told him, much to his surprise, "but I know what you are about, and be warned it cannot succeed. I shall be watching and waiting."

She walked away from him briskly, but he was fast in pursuit. "What do you mean by that remark, Miss Winterton?"

"Am I no longer Davinia?" she asked archly. "You exhibited rather more charm a while ago."

"Dammit, woman, what are you about?"

Shaken by his sudden anger, Davinia realised at last she was playing a dangerous game. If Mr Monkswood was to be believed, the marquis was ruthless and without conscience and she would be safer to remember that at all times.

She averted her gaze from his probing look. "It is of no account. I am making a cake of myself and I beg you not to heed so foolish a woman."

"I cannot agree you are foolish. You can never be that."

"Such flattery, my lord, is like to turn my head," she responded, adopting once more a flirtatious attitude which she knew must confuse him.

"*Chéri.*" Mademoiselle du Plessy's plaintive cry was unmistakable.

"Hell and damnation!" the marquis swore as he turned to his bride-to-be who once more cast Davinia the darkest of looks as she smiled beguilingly at Lord Ravelston.

"The shoot is about to begin, *chéri*. You would not wish to be left behind, *n'est-ce pas*?"

"Naturally not," he replied, still frowning darkly. "I believe I shall join your father." He glanced at Davinia. "Why don't you join the other ladies by the river, Miss Winterton? It would be much safer there."

"What an odd word, my lord. Is it not safe here?" Her eyes were wide and innocent and she knew he was deeply angry although he could do nothing about it here in the open in the view of others.

"It can be quite dangerous when shot goes astray," he told her, speaking with quiet deliberation.

"Does that happen very often?"

"Occasionally, and sometimes with fatal results."

"Then I shall have to remain vigilant, my lord."

He strode away, moving towards the comte. Mademoiselle du Plessy looked triumphant, saying, "Really, Miss Winterton, you are quite shameless in your pursuit of my dear Ravelston. Your pursuit of him is no longer amusing, though, to either of us."

So saying she turned on her heel and flounced off in the direction the marquis had taken. Tears of frustration welled up in Davinia's eyes, but she fought them back, knowing this was not the time for self-pity, and it was of no account what Veronique du Plessy thought of her. Certainly Lord Ravelston knew she was not in pursuit of him, at least not for the reasons Veronique attributed to her. A great statesman's life was in danger and she had to avert a tragedy taking place.

She followed in the wake of the others, along the river bank. Flocks of duck flew overhead, the salvos of shot drowning out the beating of their wings. Now and again the marquis cast her a furious look, but she affected not to see it. She hardly dare take her eyes off him and when she did it was to stare at Lord Castlereagh who appeared quite unconcerned although Mr Monkswood's unease was very evident.

He held tightly on to his gun although he didn't attempt to discharge it in the air.

In normal circumstances she might have marvelled at the fact that the marquis was such an excellent shot, but on this occasion Davinia was only filled with foreboding. Thunder rumbled in the distance as the sky grew more black and she hoped that the shoot would have to be called off before calamity struck.

"Do you find this diverting?" the marquis asked in a harsh whisper during a lull as his gun was loaded.

"Your unerring eye is a marvel to behold," she replied, tossing her head back.

"Why not try beholding someone else?" he suggested in a pleasant enough voice before snatching his gun from the loader and striding away from her.

Davinia hung back as the party waited patiently for more duck to appear over the river. The rumbling of thunder was causing flocks of them to rise up in flight. It couldn't have been better.

She watched resentfully as the marquis raised his fowling piece to bring down a duck with one unerring shot. Lord Kirkland fired, too, and then Lord Castlereagh. One volley followed closely on another. Davinia was scarcely aware of the noise as she surveyed them all in turn. As she did so her gaze suddenly became riveted upon the Comte du Plessy who had moved forward to take his shot. However, his gun was not pointing upwards towards the flock of birds overhead but towards an unsuspecting Lord Castlereagh. For a long moment Davinia stared at him in disbelief. Everyone else was concentrating on the birds flying overhead, even Lord Ravelston. Suddenly he, too, began to turn and Davinia knew then how mistaken she had been. She saw the look of horror on the marquis's face as the comte took careful aim. It all happened in the space of a split second.

Before the marquis could move, uttering a cry of warning, Davinia leaped forward. The Frenchman was startled and half turned towards her, at the same time as the shot was discharged from the gun. She saw Lord Ravelston push the Minister for War out of the way just as a ferocious pain seared her arm. It was enough to make her cry out as she stumbled and fell to the ground.

Pandemonium seemed to have broken out all around. People thundered about all around her, most of them looking totally bewildered. The cold from the mud beneath her began to permeate Davinia's thin gown as a dear, familiar voice cried, "Davinia!"

Another shot echoed out, followed by a growl of thunder. Fire seemed to have engulfed her arm. Somewhere nearby a woman was screaming loudly. Davinia knew it was not her own screams. All she could manage was a low moan.

The marquis's face loomed over her. "Davinia. Davinia, my love. Speak to me, I beg of you. Give me a word as a sign."

"I love you," she gasped and then mercifully remembered no more.

PART THREE

Aftermath

[142]

THIRTEEN

Lady Kirkland appeared to be exceedingly happy. Davinia blinked and looked at her blankly wondering what had caused her such pleasure. Davinia sensed immediately that something out of the ordinary had occurred, but for the moment could not think what it might be.

"Lady Kirkland, what has happened?"

"Oh, I am so pleased you are much improved," the countess declared. "We have been so worried for you."

Davinia realised then that she was lying in her own bed with Mira sitting at one side and Lady Kirkland at the other. The countess leaned forward to mop Davinia's brow gently with her own special eau de cologne made up for her in Pall Mall.

As Davinia attempted to move, a pain seared through her body. "My arm," she gasped, falling back into the pillows. "Oh, I remember it all now! The comte. Lord Castlereagh!"

"He is safe, never you fear."

"And my arm?" Davinia asked fearfully.

"It will mend, my dear. The shot merely grazed the flesh but you contracted a fever which caused us great concern. However, you are now much improved and Dr Foster is well pleased with you."

Remembering the events that had almost ended her life, tears sprang to Davinia's eyes. That and the injustice of her earlier thoughts of Lord Ravelston. At that moment she felt she could bear anything in the future now she knew he was blameless.

"What happened?" she asked again. "I'm so confused. I believe I swooned."

"You were not alone in that." Lady Kirkland sighed and looked across at her maid. "Fetch some calf's foot jelly for Miss Winterton, Mira. It is all ready and prepared in the kitchen."

When the maid had gone Lady Kirkland revealed, "Lord Castlereagh is most grateful to you for your heroism. He has left a note expressing his gratitude and that of Lady Castlereagh. I shall let you have it later."

Davinia put her one good hand to her brow. "Is he truly safe?"

"Oh, yes, indeed, thanks to you, my dear. I am very proud of you and so, may I add, is Kirkland."

"Have the Castlereaghs gone from here?"

"Several days ago. Matters of state necessitated his departure even if this unfortunate incident had not happened, but he did ask to be kept informed of your progress. All my guests have now left, although several did remain until they were certain of your recovery—the Henleys and the Grindles. They were most concerned as we all were."

"Lord Ravelston?" she could not resist asking.

The countess's manner became more restrained. "He was obliged to escort Mademoiselle du Plessy to some of her friends. It was necessary for him to take her away from here as soon as was possible." She hesitated before adding, "I don't know how much you recall . . ."

"Very little after the comte discharged the shot. There was a good deal of noise, I recall."

The countess sighed again. "There seems no advantage in hiding from you the fact that the comte turned the gun upon himself the moment he realised the attempt on Lord Castlereagh's life had failed. He knew then he was all dished up. Only the gibbet awaited him. It must have seemed the easiest way for him.''

Tears came to Davinia's eyes once more. ''I thought Lord Ravelston was the traitor.''

Lady Kirkland laughed harshly. ''What faddle! Ravelston has a heart as true as oak. It was he who was engaged in guarding Lord Castlereagh.''

''Did you know of that all the while?''

''No! Even though I have known Ravelston since he was a boy I had no notion! I regarded him as a Corinthian dedicated to nought but pleasure. Only Mr Monkswood and Lord Castlereagh himself were privy to the risk. Oh, and Emily, too. Poor woman. She must have been exceeding concerned for him. The threat had been in operation for months.''

''Lady Castlereagh,'' Davinia whispered, almost to herself.

''Ravelston even slept in her dressing room so he could guard them the better. Imagine!''

Davinia smiled. ''I have no need to, my lady.''

Mira returned with the calf's foot jelly, which Lady Kirkland insisted upon feeding to her companion. ''I shall answer no more questions until this has been eaten,'' she declared, and Davinia had no option but to obey.

''La! There was a time I thought you would never recover.''

When Lizzie Moncrieff came breezing into the small drawing room, Davinia had been reading, for the umpteenth time, Lord Castlereagh's missive.

The girl peered at her anxiously. ''I own you do look less peaked now. Mama has been so strict in keeping me away when I was so anxious to have a coze with you.''

''I beg your pardon if I kept you waiting.''

She sat down on a comfortable bergere chair and leaned forward with a confidential air. ''I have never been so mortified. Imagine! I was playing hide and seek with Samuel Livesey when all the excitement took place.''

With her one good hand Davinia contrived to fold the parchment and push it under a book which stood on a nearby table. ''You were well away from it all, Miss Moncrieff. Only see what has happened to me.''

''I'd as lief risk a shot in my arm as miss the greatest diversion I am ever like to witness.''

''You are as ever foolish, my dear.''

The girl was not put out by Davinia's scolding and she smiled good-naturedly. ''I scarce think you should be censuring me after what you did. Nothing can be more foolhardy than acting in so precipitate a fashion.''

''I wouldn't dream of arguing with you on that score. Pray tell me what day it is. I am still a trifle confused.''

''Sunday.''

Davinia's eyes grew wide. ''Why, it happened days ago! I had no notion so much time has passed and yet it might have been years ago.''

''Mr Kingston has declared his intention of visiting you after church today,'' Lizzie confided gleefully. ''What a pity you were insensible to all the fuss and botheration. It was more than you are ever like to attract in your entire life.'' Davinia cast her a wry look as the girl went on, ''Ravel was quite beside himself, Miss Winterton. He insisted on carrying you back to the carriage and then into the house himself. I thought he was bound to have apoplexy before the physician arrived. He was persuaded you had been given notice to quit. I suspect he is not as disinterested in you as you might believe, although that is no rare distinction.''

Davinia's mind was far away, returning to that hazy moment when she had fallen to the ground. *My love,* he had said. But as Lizzie had pointed out it was no rare distinction to be the object of Lord Ravelston's affection.

"I gave him a set-down, you may be sure," the girl went on to say in a pert manner.

"Why?"

"Because of all his secrecy. Fancy his being as close as oak with *me*. It is mortifying."

"You must see it was necessary. It could scarce become the object of drawing room *on-dits*."

"I have already forgiven him, you may be sure," the girl said with magnanimity. "I always considered Monsieur du Plessy a quiz, but I was bound to pity Mademoiselle du Plessy. She had an immediate attack of the vapours."

"I shouldn't wonder," Davinia answered darkly, her own heart heavy for the girl's sake.

"It seems she knew nothing of her papa's wickedness and Mira was bound to burn feathers although finally Dr Foster was called upon to administer a nostrum. You would have thought *she* had been shot, not you. It is Ravelston I pity now. Mama says that because she is innocent of all implication he will be honour-bound to marry her. The comte must have been as cunning as a dead pig to think he could succeed in assassinating Lord Castlereagh."

"On the contrary, Miss Moncrieff, he was exceeding clever, I believe, for he almost did succeed."

"Mama is mortified that she harboured such a viper under her roof, but Lord Kirkland has reminded her it was only because Mademoiselle du Plessy was Ravelston's bride-to-be. No other consideration would have led Mama to include them in the house party. This will be the undoing of Ravel, Miss Winterton. Only fancy, when he is leg-shackled to that creature, he will not dare to show his face anywhere in Society. She will be an outcast and he will be obliged to become one, too."

"All the same, I am persuaded that consideration will not lead him to abandon her."

"Oh, indeed, and I am as mad as a weaver whenever I

think of it. He has such principle. No man—and certainly not one as fine as he—should be obliged to suffer hardship.''

''I suppose we must be thankful that all has ended as well as it has,'' Davinia ventured, sounding a mite unconvinced of the fact.

Even news of Ravelston's concern for her was not cheering. In the circumstances it would be natural, and she didn't doubt his concern for Veronique du Plessy would be even greater whatever her father's crime.

''I am in a fidge to know the entire story,'' Lizzie went on, ''but I don't suppose we shall until we see Ravel again.''

Davinia sat up on the day bed. The pain in her arm had dulled to an ache which did not trouble her often. ''Are we like to do so soon?''

The girl shrugged her thin shoulders. ''I cannot say. Nor does Mama know, but it is evident Ravel has been working secretly for the government ever since he resigned his commission in the army. Everything is still in such a muddle. We have heard nothing from London.''

The door opened slightly and then, after a moment's hesitation, fully to admit Lady Kirkland. ''Lizzie!'' she scolded. ''I trust you do not trouble Miss Winterton's head too much.''

''No, Mama,'' the girl replied, grinning at Davinia as she spoke. ''I am merely divulging the latest *on-dits* to divert Miss Winterton's mind from her injury.''

''There is little enough tattle to impart,'' the countess replied. ''After what occurred here last week I am more than relieved it is so. I shall be reluctant to hold another house party you may be certain.''

''Oh, Mama,'' Lizzie scoffed, ''you know that isn't true. You enjoy it all so much.''

Lady Kirkland sighed and it was evident the events of the past week had affected her deeply. ''Well, we must now think ahead to Lizzie's Season, and all it will involve.

Mantua-makers, milliners, caterers and florists for the come-out ball. It will be a welcome diversion, I must confess.'' She glanced at Davinia then. ''At least when we remove to London it will divert *your* mind from the awful experience of this week.''

As the countess smiled at her reassuringly Davinia was not so certain. The marquis was lost to her for ever, honourbound to marry a traitor's daughter. No amount of social activity could erase the thought of that from her mind, or the sorrow from her heart.

Summer was enjoying its last blaze of glory before autumn began to encroach. Two figures, gowned in muslin, one in white and one in buttercup yellow, were passing through the garden, snipping at the rosebuds as they went.

Lizzie Moncrieff held the trug as Davinia cut the roses. ''I wonder if Lord Kirkland is enjoying his grouse shooting,'' the girl pondered. ''I know Mama was looking forward to going to Yorkshire, but the house is sadly quiet without her.''

Davinia laughed. ''How true that is, but it will not be for much longer.''

''Is it only next week when we all remove to London?''

''Yes, indeed,'' Davinia replied, laughing again, for the girl often mentioned the event.

''I shall begin to plan my wardrobe for the Season. I do believe I shall find it pleasing after all.''

''Of course you will,'' Davinia told her.

''Do you feel robust enough for the journey, Miss Winterton?''

''Never more so. You need harbour no worries on that score.''

''How shall you like it there, I wonder? You are quite unused to life in Town.''

Davinia smiled faintly as she snipped at a stem. The prospect of theatres, routs and pleasure gardens, which once sounded to be wondrous, did not much attract her of late.

"It is my duty to go wherever Lady Kirkland wishes."

Lizzie looked impish. "Mayhap you will regret leaving Thomas Kingston behind. He has been very attentive since your accident."

"Mr Kingston has merely been executing his duty. Visiting the sick of this parish is a part of his work."

"No one believes it is so in your case, and if you are known to be going away, it might just be the thing to bring him up to scratch."

"Oh, Miss Moncrieff, I beg of you not to speak of it," Davinia replied, looking away in distress.

"You are too modest; I have always said so. The man is evidently moonstruck and you may be sure I shall remind him that you are about to leave, next time he happens to call which will be soon, have no doubt."

Davinia gasped. "Miss Moncrieff, I forbid you to do any such thing!"

When Lizzie made no reply Davinia turned around again to see the girl had run across the lawn and was in joyful conversation with Lord Ravelston.

Davinia's heart began to beat faster and she was unable to move from the spot. The sight of him caused her misery and gladness in equal measure. Unthinkingly she clutched a rose to her breast as she watched him and the girl in conversation. After a few moments Lizzie cast him a wry look and ran back towards the house, the trug in her hand. There was a faint smile on his face as he watched her go before looking across the expanse of green to where Davinia was still standing.

He was hatless but still wore his driving coat and it was evident he had only just arrived. Still holding the rose, she began to walk towards him and all the while he never took his eyes from her.

"I came back as soon as I was able," he told her when she was close enough to hear.

Davinia affected a careless smile. "It is very good of you to trouble, my lord. We certainly did not look to see you here so soon."

"You look very robust, which is a great pleasure after the last time I saw you. How is your arm?"

"Entirely better." She demonstrated the fact by moving it briskly.

"I'm so relieved to see it." When she moved away from him because his presence all at once discomforted her, he asked, "May I walk with you for a while?"

"If you wish."

They began to walk across the lawn and as they set off he confided, "Lord Castlereagh has charged me to convey his heartfelt thanks to you."

"There is no need. I have already received a note from him, which, in truth, was entirely unnecessary. I am happy to have been of service to so great a man."

"That was a task allotted to me. I was well aware of the danger and I should not have allowed my attention to stray, even for so short a time. Had any worse fate befallen you I should never have forgiven myself."

She looked up at him. "No one could hold you to blame."

"It is very magnanimous of you to say so." After a moment's hesitation he asked, "Will you allow me to explain the circumstances now that I am at liberty to do so?"

"I am all curiosity, my lord. There is so much about the matter we still do not know."

"You once accused me of lying faster than a dog can trot. . . ."

She laughed uncomfortably. "You must not remind me of my foolishness."

"That was not my purpose, and you spoke only the truth.

There is nothing foolish about that. I have told many a false-hood, and it has often grieved me to do so.''

"I do understand your reasons," she answered primly. "Your work has been, of necessity, a matter of secrecy."

"Your understanding and generosity is very welcome, ma'am." He paused for a moment before going on, "Last winter when you gave me shelter, I had not been the recipi-ent of the wrath of a cuckolded husband. A day or so previ-ously I had received some information from an agent of the government who had recently returned from France. It con-cerned a plot to assassinate the new Minister for War. If it had succeeded it would have turned our own war effort into total chaos. I don't doubt Boney would have then been able to implement his invasion plan."

"How dreadful!" Davinia gasped.

"The agent told me all he had learned, including the name of a man suspected of being implicated. The informa-tion was imparted to me only just in time, for shortly after-wards the man was done to death.''

Again Davinia gasped. "How shocking," adding in a softer voice, "and I misjudged you so greatly."

He smiled faintly. "You judged me only on the way I al-lowed you to see me. No blame can be attached to you.''

"The men who attacked you . . . ?''

"The very same men who killed my informant. I was pur-sued, attacked and then left for dead. It was, however, to my ultimate advantage that they believed me dead, for it would then be assumed their wicked plan was safe to pursue. For-tunately they did not know my true identity and the comte, when I made his acquaintance, was unaware of my purpose. After I had been nursed back to health by your good self, I was able to impart my information to the authorities in Lon-don. Since then I have endeavoured to remain close to the man I believed would make the attempt on Lord Castle-reagh's life.''

"So you knew it was he all the time?" He nodded grimly

and she asked, "Why, oh, why did he do it? It is quite incomprehensible to me."

"I'm given to understand he was promised the return of his fortune and estates."

She was immediately angry. "What an abominable way to serve a country which has afforded him a welcome and safety!" After a moment she asked hesitantly, not daring to look at him, "How . . . how is Mademoiselle du Plessy?"

"Quite distraught and inconsolable, I'm afraid. The shock has affected her grievously. I have placed her with some good people at Brighton in the hope that she might recover her spirits before too long."

"I am so sorry," Davinia said with true feeling.

He looked grim. "You are uncommonly generous."

"She is blameless, and her situation is now so pitiable."

He stopped walking and turned abruptly to face her. "Do you recall what you said to me after you were shot?"

She had to look away, twisting the stem of the rose between her fingers. "It was all a good deal chaotic," she murmured.

"You need not hesitate to admit it; Mademoiselle du Plessy has relieved me of all obligation to her." She looked at him then with hope as he added, "I am free to say I have loved you for a very long time. It has been agony to have to hide my true feelings for you, moreover act the part of a man you were bound to despise. Do I dare to hope you might harbour some small affection for me after all?"

In a moment she was enfolded in his arms, her face pressed against his broadcloth coat. "My love," she murmured, "my dearest love."

He held her away. "Will you marry me?"

"Mar . . . ry," she stammered, her heart beating wildly, for it had all happened so fast. Her head was in a whirl. "I hadn't thought . . ."

"I dared not think of it either. It would have been foolhardy to allow myself to think of you, for it was probable I would never be able to reveal my love for you. Veronique . . ."

Davinia averted her face from his. "Did you love her very much?"

"Heaven forgive me, I did not love her at all. Davinia, paying court to her was an easy way into her father's confidence, but Veronique is a very determined young woman and an offer of marriage was expected of me. I delayed it as long as I could; to do so further would have placed my position at risk. I am far from proud of what I did."

"You had little choice in the matter, but you might have been obliged to marry her."

"Yes," he answered heavily, and she realised at last how far he was willing to sacrifice himself in the service of his country. "No one is more aware of that than I." Then he added, more brightly, "Do you recall the old witch's prophecy that day?"

"Hannah Endeacott. I recall it well. I shall never forget a moment spent with you."

"Then you must recall she told you of a house of grey stone with turrets and an eagle on the gates."

She laughed. "I remember. You were so scornful."

"More like afraid, for the house she described is Brookfield, my home. I knew then that your future and mine were bound together in some way. At that time, though, it would have been foolhardy even to dream of it, and that is what angered me."

"She warned of a danger, too," Davinia recalled, shuddering slightly and he drew close again. "Oh, Rupert, I do love you, but shall I be able to endure the pain of knowing you might be put in the way of such terrible danger again in the future?"

"I promise you it is no longer so. Although the matter of the comte's death is being spoken of as a hunting accident, and your heroic act will never become public knowledge, it has been decided I shall not in future be engaged in that kind of government business. The secrecy of my position can no longer be guaranteed—many here that day will have guessed my role—so my usefulness is at an end.''

Davinia drew a sigh of profound relief. ''Are you very sorry about that?''

''There was a time when I sought only diversion and adventure,'' he replied, looking down into her eyes, ''but now I have found something so much better I wouldn't wish for anything to jeopardise it.''

She blushed again and murmured, ''Do you not fear life will become tedious?''

He laughed then. ''With you at my side it could never be that.''

He kissed her again, longingly and passionately, before putting his arm around her waist, drawing her close to him. They walked in the bright summer sunshine towards the future that awaited them, together at last.

More romance from Regency and...

RACHELLE EDWARDS

By the year 2000, 2 out of 3 Americans could be illiterate.

It's true.

Today, 75 million adults...about one American in three, can't read adequately. And by the year 2000, U.S. News & World Report envisions an America with a literacy rate of only 30%.

Before that America comes to be, you can stop it...by joining the fight against illiteracy today.

Call the Coalition for Literacy at toll-free **1-800-228-8813** and volunteer.

**Volunteer
Against Illiteracy.
The only degree you need
is a degree of caring.**

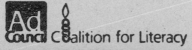

Ad Council   Coalition for Literacy   LV-2